Also by Amelia Gray

THREATS

Museum of the Weird

AM/PM

Gutshot

Gutshot

STORIES

Amelia Gray

FARRAR, STRAUS AND GIROUX   NEW YORK

Farrar, Straus and Giroux
18 West 18th Street, New York 10011

Library of Congress Cataloging-in-Publication Data
Gray, Amelia, 1982–
    [Short stories. Selections]
    Gutshot : stories / Amelia Gray. — First edition.
       pages ;   cm
    ISBN 978-0-374-17544-3 (softcover) — ISBN 978-0-374-71257-0 (ebook)
    I. Title.

  PS3607 .R387A6 2015
  813'.6—dc23

                                                        2014031210

Designed by Abby Kagan

Farrar, Straus and Giroux books may be purchased for educational, business,
or promotional use. For information on bulk purchases, please contact the
Macmillan Corporate and Premium Sales Department at 1-800-221-7945,
extension 5442, or write to specialmarkets@macmillan.com.

www.fsgbooks.com
www.twitter.com/fsgbooks • www.facebook.com/fsgbooks

10 9 8 7 6 5 4 3 2 1

For Susan Quesal

Contents

One

Two

Three

Four

CONTENTS

Five

One

In the Moment

It had been a memorable date after such a long line of failures. Turns out they had hidden the same punk tapes in their closets as teenagers and had always secretly wanted to work as photographers for nature magazines. Neither had been to Europe and both dropped an ice cube in their morning cup of coffee. Her name was Emily, a name she hated, but Mark found it reminded him of reading picture books with a flashlight under the covers of his childhood bed. Emily was the name of a girl hero whose intrepid adventures took her around the world and even underground.

It was a far better name, anyway, than Mark, a name that regularly conjured the image of a bucket of black paint thrown against a prison wall. They were both morally but not financially satisfied with their current mid-level organizational positions—they had discussed the subject at length the week before during the nonprofit conference where they met—and hoped to strike out on their own someday, individually. "Or together," Mark said, raising his glass.

"I was hoping you would come up," she said, once they were outside her apartment.

"Boy howdy," he said. And so began their first evening together, in the elevator and then tumbling over the bed and in a pile of her clean laundry, and later, unpleasantly wedged between the oven and the refrigerator in a move she claimed was solely for luck. He was fascinated by her textures: a rough spot on the side meat of her buttock; a thin rumpled place on the back of her hand where she had burned herself with oil. She had a little round mass the size of a ball bearing in her left breast. All of this was new to Mark and he was glad to experience it.

"Your body is tremendous," she said after. He didn't feel that his body was much beyond a device that propelled him from breakfast to dinner—it featured a growing paunch and a knee that tricked up before wet weather—and he nearly told her so before realizing that she was happy with him and trying to be kind, and it had been so long since a woman had tried to be kind with him that he was immediately lulled into peace with her, and they fell asleep right there in the bathtub.

A series of successful dates followed. They decided that when they were old, they would buy an RV and take it around the country to attend garlic festivals and state fairs. She brought a bale of fresh hay home from the farmers' market so they could experience what it felt like to take a roll in it. Mark realized in short order that he loved Emily and that he was afraid to lose her, and the two thoughts abutted unpleasantly and spoiled an entire evening because he couldn't eat his dinner for watching her and then fainted getting into the cab and woke up in her living room, confessing his fears while she held a damp cloth against his forehead.

"We are connected in this manner and I am afraid," he was saying.

"You must practice the act of connection without attachment," she said. "Think of us as two stones together at the bottom of a shallow stream. We jostle against each other." She pushed him gently on the shoulder to illustrate the concept of jostling. "Eventually the stream pulls us apart, or covers us with a fine silt."

"That seems bad."

"When you truly understand it, it will remove all suffering." She dropped the cloth into a bowl of cool water she had prepared. His limbs were too heavy to reach for her and so she stripped him from the waist down right there on the couch and did all the work. Her breast brushed against his cheek and he visualized the lump inside as a pebble in a stream, which he might observe without attachment.

They made dinners and vacation plans and he moved his things into her apartment. Mark felt closer to Emily than he had felt to any other person living or dead since grade school, when he and a group of boys formed a secret society in the woods behind the Dairy Queen. He tried to imagine being eight years old, there in the woods, and projected himself into his younger body and mind. He tried to tell that boy that not thirty years later he would meet a woman who would give him such a feeling of peace. The young boy listened and then called his older self a gaylord and Mark said Fair enough, Young Mark, I have become a Gaylord of Love.

He went to the mall and bought Emily a pendant on a long silver chain and presented it to her and recited the chorus of a Fleetwood Mac song that dealt chiefly with the concept of running into the shadows, and Emily put the necklace on and said it was fine.

He liked to cook and she took out the trash. They both cleaned the bathtub on occasion. It was a pretty good setup. Whenever he faced a problem at work, for example when his coworker came back from England and put a poster of Stonehenge up over the window and Mark could no longer see the street, Emily taught him to view each day as a wild element divorced from past and future. He needed not to exist as a point on a vector but ultimately to destroy the vector and inhabit that solitary point, like living inside a meteor without fear or knowledge of its movement. If he could place himself in the moment of sitting in the office without recalling the view from the window or anticipating a morning where he felt sick with desire for the pleasure of simple natural light, he might see that the poster threw a greenish shade over his cubicle corner and gave the impression that he was working under a pane of stained glass.

"But then I'd have to remember a time I stood before a church window," he said, "thereby entering the past."

"That is not what this is about," she said, and he saw that she was right, because he couldn't remember what any of it was about. They were watching Korean-language television at the time. A problem with the cable provider resulted in them only receiving Korean-language television, but after a few disorienting days they found it was comforting to observe the dramas without context and they watched them as children watch adults, taking cues from laughing or weeping and then mirroring the gestures.

Later that week, he forgot that they had gone grocery shopping and returned home with a bag of plums to add to a rotting pile of nectarines. He left it all there, determined to understand their use. Cartons of eggs stacked up in the fridge and she speculated that she could make a quiche but she had distanced herself mentally from any recipe and so cracked the eggs in a pan and poked them listlessly on the stove until they burned and had to be thrown out.

"We should go out with our friends this weekend," he said.

"We don't have friends," she said.

The house phone rang and he picked it up. "Is my daughter there?" a woman asked, Mark realized after a moment, in English.

"Who is your daughter?"

"Emily is my daughter," she said. "Are you her new boyfriend?"

He was quiet, turning over the idea that Emily had a mother. He imagined a whole gloomy family tree, and then imagined taking a chain saw to the tree and sitting on the stump, listening to Fleetwood Mac on a cassette player and waiting for the wood to dry so he could burn it. He pulled the phone out of the wall and threw it in the recycling and then he picked it out of the recycling and put it in the trash.

She followed his lead on clearing the place and at turns brought out to the curb a jar of olives, curtain rods, ice cube trays, an electric guitar, a vacuum cleaner, silverware, her baby pictures, a bag of shampoos collected from hotel rooms, and the hay from the farmers' market, which she stuffed into three paper bags. She hired men to remove the couch and the TV and when she had no cash for payment they additionally removed a box of jewelry.

At work, he stood with his nose to the Stonehenge poster until a woman from Human Resources asked him if he might like to take a walk with her. She said that his performance had been going sideways lately and that they were looking for someone moving in more of a vertical direction. The words coming out of her mouth didn't make sense and Mark tried taking context clues from the pictures of children and mountains set in frames on her desk. Before she outlined his severance package, she had to ask him to stop chanting.

The walk home was deeply satisfying, so ideal in the movements of the small animals and in the appearance of flaws in the road. Even the flaws, on further observation, were so perfectly placed that they stood as proof of a grand design created for his witness. He sat down on the sidewalk to observe the way a banner flapped beneath a store awning and stayed there for a few hours, leaning against a mailbox.

He returned home to find Emily sitting on a milk crate in the middle of their empty apartment. She was naked from the waist up and examining her bra. "What do you think this is?" she asked, turning the cup so he could observe the flecks of dried blood inside it.

"I have no idea." And indeed, though he searched his memory, all he turned up were strange pictures out of place: a hornet alighting on the upper corner of his crib and disgorging the first papered layer of its nest; a woman kneeling before a man, both robed in white; a boy seeming to leap from his bike onto the hood of a passing car. "I can't even imagine."

House Heart

The home remains. Even if the house was razed, the foundation scored and broken, and the pieces carried away, there would be a feeling of home, where people cooked dinner or lay down exhausted or looked out the window at the garbage truck rumbling down the road.

Our home was once the preparation wing of a garment factory, in which material was boiled with chemicals to change its color and character. We found this information in public records, though hints were present in the scars on the concrete where machines were once bolted, an industrial ventilation system like an artery across the high, open ceiling, feeding air to each white-walled room. The larger silo has since been destroyed and replaced with a new shopping complex, but our home remains, a testament to utility.

It was my idea to rent the girl. My partner called a service and asked the receptionist if their business practices included the concept of fair trade. It was important to him as a consumer, and the least he could do would be to utilize his privilege to benefit others, even in some small way. As he spoke, I rubbed the crotch of his jeans.

The girl arrived the next morning and rang the bell twice while we took turns admiring her through the peephole. She read our address from a pink notebook. Her hair was blond and ironed straight and she was falsely tanned. She leaned back to look up and down the street, shading her eyes with the book. While we watched her, my partner asked me if we could educate her on the physical dangers of using chemically bleached products and I said No, none of that.

The girl pounded on our door with her little fist, examining the peephole. We could see her eyes, pale and clear, the whites like water in a dish. It occurred to me that men delivered our groceries and laundry, our products, and this was the first girl I had seen in a year, at least. She looked surprised, shocked even, when my partner unlocked the door and she saw us both standing there, smiling at her, but she entered our home anyway and put down her things.

She said she had just come from class and I asked her what class she was taking and she said Life science and I said Ah, yes. Her fingers were manicured with a pink polish. She smelled like a bowl of sugar that had been sprayed with a disinfectant. Even her name sounded processed. My partner clasped the girl's shoulders and told her that he was happy she had come. She started to say something but he embraced her and she frowned and put her tanned arms across his back and said Okay, okay.

My partner suggested that she change into something more comfortable. We led her to the bathroom and she removed her dress before us on the hemp bathmat and stood quietly while we anointed her with oils. I rubbed her feet and legs and my partner did her back. The oil was a jojoba blend to which I had added fresh sage and rosemary. She was tense under my hands. There seemed to be a thin layer of glowing light just under her skin, a scratch away. I began to feel calmer as I rubbed and was able to hear more of the conversation my partner was having with the girl. He talked about how honored we were that she joined us on her journey through life. He asked her the question he had read that morning on his Questions calendar, which was What are you doing to make life more beautiful for the next generation? She said she wanted to be a physical therapist. He moaned a little.

The preparations over, he led the way to the air-conditioner intake duct in the hallway. I passed him a screwdriver and he began to remove the duct's grate, handing me the small screws. He said that becoming a physical therapist was very much like playing House Heart with someone you trust. She said that she didn't understand. She stood between us with her arms crossed over her breasts, each hand holding the opposite shoulder. The oil made a small pool around her toes. I held her hips and kissed her face and tried to tell her a joke but she didn't laugh. She asked what we were doing in the hallway and I told her that my partner and I have a game we like to play and it's a special game to us, very special, but we never have had a chance to share it with someone else, and it would mean so much for us to take that step with her help. He was prying the grate from its spot and so I hushed the girl and patted her round bottom.

The duct's main supply area was large enough for a crouching man to spend a few productive hours on the controls behind locked panels inside. There would be plenty of space for our girl. When we kissed her and coaxed her in, she barely had to bow her head and then stood comfortably. Her feet were bare but I had swept the spot many times before, and that morning had scrubbed it clean with a vinegar-soaked rag. When my partner moved to affix the grate she made a whine of protest, but he explained that sealing her inside would allow us to truly play the game, and that we would be so pleased if she would help us finally achieve this milestone as a couple, a romantic goal for which she would be well compensated, enough to focus on her studies for the remainder of the year. Finally she was silent and the grate was quickly secured.

For a while, nothing happened. I worried for a moment that she had vanished. Then we heard her scraping around, feeling the boundaries with her feet and hands, no doubt discovering there wasn't room for her to sit. My partner said that she would find a duct at her head and one at her feet. Those main lines would branch into smaller channels leading to different rooms; one would end up over the kitchen and another would terminate in the living room, one over the chandelier in the dining room and the other three in the bathroom, bedroom, and office. She would be able to hear us at different points of the ductwork, thanks to the happy accidents of design that allowed for such echoes. In a small voice, the girl asked if we could maybe just let her out. I found my purse in a closet and fed a few singles through the grate. The money stayed stuck or floating there for a moment before she took it. She would have to stand there with it in her hand since she didn't have anywhere to put it.

The scratching continued, the thumps of her body bracing against a confined space, then a sharp kick against the metal. She was crying softly. My partner knocked on the wall and told her to calm herself, that she would earn five times more than she would if she had made love to us in a traditional way. He said there was no danger to playing House Heart, that there were secrets to be found.

Her noises became more frantic as she felt along the

corridor. We heard her clamber up to the high duct, finding a place for her bare feet in the metal's slim niches. She had stopped crying, the effort of movement distracting her enough to focus on her task. I put my eye to the grate and saw her legs dangling before they vanished upward. My partner held my hips and we did it right there in the hallway. We licked each other's faces, listening to the girl above us. At that moment, she was learning that she could crawl on her hands and knees in the main passage, but that in the smaller lines, she would have to slide on her belly, arms outstretched, pulling herself forward blind. At the system's smallest points, it would surround and press her from all angles.

After we were finished in the hall, we retired to the bedroom, where he rubbed some of the jojoba oil into my breasts. He rolled out of bed, arranged a stepladder under the vent, and stretched up to feed cash through the grate. He knocked on it so she would know. After a few minutes, the money disappeared and we heard her moving backward, the metal shuddering above us. I dipped my head down onto my partner's genital, savoring the girl's energy as I worked. Once I was finished, he handed me a warm towel and began his preparations for work.

My mind was once diseased with the strange and heady ambition that I might somehow improve the world by living in it. The reality of the world ruined this ideal; or rather, the fantasy of the ideal ruined its reality. It took some time to soothe myself from this truth. Eventually I found that keeping close to home and pursuing a daily practice helped to ease the stress. Making terms with my lack of true utility required a kind of physical therapy, as if I were treating a sprained ankle.

This was my daily practice: I would throw open a door and imagine the ideal world. Opening the pantry, I might declare what a fine day it was, how the morning sun glinted so kindly off available glinting things. At the door to the bedroom, I spoke of a green and placid lawn. I held out my palm in a closet and noted that it was about to rain. It was soothing. I practiced with the doors after my partner left for work. As I opened and closed the medicine cabinet, I wondered idly if the girl had a partner of her own. Seeing as we hadn't heard from her employer, it was safe to assume she was alone. I took only slight pleasure from this.

The girl slept up there each night, turning over every few hours. There would be no space for her to curl her legs up to her chest. One night, my partner left the bed and I heard him whispering to her in the bathroom. In the morning, we heard her noises change as she lifted her elbows and slid on her belly. My partner rolled atop me and said that the girl had begun to trust the surfaces she was coming to know. It was very exciting for him, which made it very exciting for me.

He left for work and I opened and closed a cabinet for a while before putting on water for tea. I could hear the girl rumble above me in the kitchen. She said Could you let me out of here? I replied that the world which had been created for her was out of my control. She said it wasn't true, that if I might call an authority, everything would be solved.

An insolent silence followed. Pushing aside my desire to cut the duct open with one of the heavy steak knives and plunge the knife into her neck, I pointed out that she had made all the choices that brought her to that moment, that if she had been forced to do anything in her life, it had not been in our presence and we would not be held accountable. As I spoke, a drop landed on my shoulder. She confessed that she had wanted to be let out because she didn't know where else to use the toilet. I took my tea into the living room, annoyed. She banged away for a while but eventually calmed down. A few hours passed and I cleaned the mess from where it had landed on the kitchen floor.

From then on, she made waste in that area, directly over the stove. We couldn't convince her otherwise, even though my partner did his best to startle her as she did it, pounding the duct with a broom handle. It must have been her small idea of insurrection. My partner shouted that she was lucky to be where she was, that the world was a terrifying place for anyone and particularly terrifying for a girl like her, and that when she toughened her softer skin and grew out some more of her body hair, she might understand her own strength and power. Eventually, without a word to me about it, he rigged up a tarp and bucket under the kitchen vent. And at night, they whispered.

We were sleeping late one morning when the girl began to knock above us. We tried to ignore her with some mutual masturbation but the knocking grew louder and she cried out without words. My partner got out of bed and left the room for some time. When he returned he spoke to her, saying he had opened the vent over the study and left his watch inside. She stopped knocking and slid away.

It was his father's watch, I knew. The man would drive his family cross-country every few months to observe the passing seasons. They watched leaves and local rock formations and various beaches, blissfully unaware of the part they were taking in the destruction of the very environment they enjoyed. He drank gas station coffee from Styrofoam cups and when he finished the coffee, he would bite into the cup itself, chewing it thoughtfully, usually consuming the whole thing before the next destination. On one of his later birthdays, he bought himself a fine watch and enjoyed it for a few years before he died. It was one of those things that my partner had long wanted to get rid of without knowing exactly why, along with his own graduation photos and a motorcycle helmet he had acquired from a friend.

A scraping noise from the far side of the house meant that she had found the watch. I imagined her spreading her fistfuls of money in front of her, slipping the watch over her thin wrist, and tucking the cash into its silver band.

That night, my partner waited until he heard my even breath and rolled from bed. I followed him and saw him unlatching the vent. He stepped in and replaced it so quietly I wouldn't have known if I hadn't watched, clutching the doorframe.

In the morning, he brought me a slab of toast with fresh butter. I could hear her above the bathroom while I washed my hair. She remarked that she heard the water running and asked if she could come down for a quick scrub. I responded that we only used baking soda and white vinegar and that I could make her a cup to take in the duct if she liked. She declined but was polite about it. She had become sweeter to me as the days wore on. I suspected she had developed a plan of winning me over through feminine duplicity. As if to corroborate this theory, the girl made her period and a few drops fell onto the floor by the bed. Every room was replete with blood-bearing potential.

While she was over the kitchen, I dragged the stepladder into the office and climbed up with a handful of radishes from the harvest box. I said that lunch was served if she could find it, that I had opened a window so we might have a little air. But I would not be fooled.

The girl created a method by which she could live with relative order. A few times a day, she would crawl into the standing-room area where she had first entered the system, finding the footholds and lowering herself. She could store her money and empty dishes there, or stand and stretch her legs. A clatter when she crawled suggested she was wearing the watch around her wrist or ankle. I listened for her while opening and closing the bathroom door, which stood next to the entry grate. My continued practice was growing strange; it was harder than ever to imagine what green grass would look like up close. My best image was of a stagnant field, like what one finds in an old pond, but even this image was fading along with my knowledge of ponds. The girl and I spoke less and less to each other.

My partner arrived home with groceries and I put them away. I prepared dinner and climbed the stepladder to serve the girl after we had eaten our share. Playing her part in the order, she ate quickly and then crawled to store her dish. Each of us had our individual function and hers was to embody the house, which had begun to smell like a hot scalp.

She had grown silent around me. I mentioned this to my partner while he was feeding me dessert. He spooned fat curds of cottage cheese into my mouth and said that it was only natural that the girl had become comfortable with her surroundings. He reminded me that I had not challenged the boundaries of my own life in many years, nor had he challenged his own. Even though we feel quite free, he remarked, every life has its surrounding wall. He wiped my chin with a napkin and kissed the napkin.

The next morning, he was in the duct with her. He must have been watching me sleep from the vent above the bed because when I woke up, he requested I replace the screws and tighten them.

He phoned the girl's employer while I was sweeping up in the kitchen. Over my noise, I could hear her say that she had decided to quit. There was a silence. At first I stopped my movement and strained to hear, but there was nothing. I tried to forget the silence and my hatred of it, opening a cabinet to put away the clean dishes.

In the back of the cabinet, over the plates, there was a portal through which I viewed the windless void of a new ecosystem. I could almost hear it breathing.

The Lark

William was a puker. His expulsions—the color, consistency, and volume of a baby's—occurred after every sentence he spoke. This unfortunate fact of life began innocently enough during his infant coos and babbles, but by the time he was barfing onto his coloring books, the doctors were stumped. He had to carry a paper cup throughout middle school. By high school he didn't have to worry about direct ridicule any longer, because he had no friends. And then everyone in his peer group graduated and left town and he was blessedly, blissfully alone.

After William was done with school he took a job at the local post office, where customers tended to be enfeebled or insane and everyone had larger problems. He would spit up into an empty soda bottle. His coworkers assumed he chewed tobacco and gave him tins of it on his birthday.

Each day at work, he stood at the counter and observed a large map of North America, which hung over the desk where folks filled out their change-of-address forms. Time passed and William began taking a daily visual interest in the Northwest Territories, which jutted down like a thumb holding Canada in its confident grasp. He imagined it as a pleasantly desolate place. On smoke breaks, he washed out his soda bottle in the bathroom sink.

One day, a woman with a wind-chapped face approached his desk. Her right arm was wrapped in a sterile bandage and she held a plastic cat carrier under her left. "What's the lark," she said.

"Beg pardon?" William said, raising the bottle to his lips.

She horked up a little something of her own. Her shoulders seemed to be coated with a thin paste. "What's the lark, what is the lark," she said.

"The lark?"

"The lark the lark," she said, inserting a fingernail under the wrapped bandage to scratch a spot.

"First-class stamps cost forty-nine cents apiece," William said. He was halfway through the sentence before he was overcome and had to grip the countertop to complete it as the bile rose. "We have some with birds on them, but I'm not sure the skylark is featured."

She hefted the cat carrier onto the counter. It registered just over thirteen pounds on the metered scale. Inside the carrier, an orange tabby let out a low warning growl. William couldn't see for certain, but it appeared as if the animal was missing all four of its legs.

"The *loork*, the lark lark the lark lake lurk lark," the woman said. She spoke with a reasonable cadence, as if she was asking about shipping rates to the Northwest Territories. William wondered briefly if perhaps she was indeed asking about shipping rates to the Northwest Territories and that his brain had transformed a reasonable question into the garble he now discerned, that he had finally lost his mind and would only hear phrases such as this until the merciful end. The cat rolled onto its side, moaning.

"Rates really depend on what you're sending," he said. He spit into the bottle and pulled a kerchief from his pocket to wipe a pearly line of drool. "If you're considering dispatching your cat, you should know that the only living thing that may be shipped via air transportation by the USPS is the queen honeybee, and that's quite an expense indeed, particularly internationally."

He had never spoken so many words in an uninterrupted spurt. A coworker looked up from behind a stack of packages. For one wild moment, William was unaffected, but before he could truly appreciate that potential, he felt it welling. He gripped the counter for support, reaching blindly for the bin. His hand found an open box and he brought it to his face before the torrent unleashed.

Customers stopped their talk to watch. His coworker covered her mouth with both hands. The material soaked the box and splashed back on his shirtfront. In it, he detected the odor of his mother's warm milk. The lark woman brayed with laughter.

William experienced the same absence of thought he always felt during the act. But because this episode lasted so much longer than usual, he found he could go further within it. He saw its bleak topography, an underwater mountain range, which revealed itself in waves of alternating anxiety and calm, the waves themselves muted and consumed. At the end, there was none of the clenched jaw and turning away that he usually felt. William realized his true freedom against the grip of time.

He saw that his unwitting target had been a box of bulk postage and he now held hundreds, if not thousands, of ruined stamps, stuck to the cardboard and each other. The box was heavy and warming at a pace that matched his rising guilt at the destruction of federal property.

The lark woman's laugh calmed to a few odd snorts. She swayed, smiling. Everyone else remained shocked beyond movement. William and the woman leaned toward each other like an old couple over a kitchen table.

"Have you ever been to Canada?" he asked.

She nodded vigorously. When she saw he was about to be sick again, she reached for him. He had a vision of her hair matted by a corona of dark ice as he readied himself to fill her cupped hands.

People of the Bay

The poet brought his people to the bay and waved for them to quiet. When they did, he said, "Build our city with wood."

The people of the bay—for they were now people of the bay—took in a shared breath. "The wood will warp and split," they said. "Our city quakes." The ground rolled a little to confirm the fact.

The poet parted the crowd to approach the loudest man, a worker who had raised his voice out of a professional concern. The poet clapped his hands on the man's shoulders.

"Raise high the cathedral walls with oak and pine," said the poet. "Make a church that becomes an ark when turned."

And so the people built the city with wood they found in the flats nearby. They built palafittes and schoolhouses and shops and a great towering wooden sanctuary. Before they had even finished these projects, the wood had already begun to split as the builder had foretold.

The poet arrived and regarded the project. He wrote something on a scroll and tucked it behind the piano, which had just been delivered on a boat. Once he was gone, the people dug out the scroll.

"Load the ark with men and women and set it to sail," someone read aloud. The people shrugged and placed the scroll back behind the piano. The earth quaked and rocked the piano, wedging it at an angle against the wall that rendered it unplayable.

Walking down the narrow road, scrolls tucked under his arm, the poet looked more like a student heading to the classroom. He arrived at the waterside and observed the palafittes. "Paint our city in blue and yellow," he said to the women setting up the bread for the morning. "Paint it to face the sun and sky, paint it to greet the bay."

The women set their mouths, but the poet remained, standing with his hands on his hips, until they took up brushes and buckets and began the slow task of painting the warping walls.

"Paint the beams thick so that when the earth quakes it

gets a mouthful of lead," the poet called out. They shooed him away. The women slopped on another coat of paint and when it dried, they repeated the process, painting so thick that the houses lost their corners.

When the poet reached the square, everyone gathered to listen. He cleared his throat and strutted haltingly across the sidewalk, looking rather like a fawn taking its first delicate steps. "Gird our quaking city with wooden beams," he cried out, his sweet voice curling through the morning air.

A murmur went up among them. "They won't hold," one said. "We'll die in our beds," shouted another. "You'll kill us!"

The poet threw back his head and looked at them one by one, his steady gaze conveying the fire in his heart. The people picked up their tools and obeyed. Underneath them all, the earth waited.

On a Pleasant Afternoon, Every Battle Is Recalled

A man should know how to butcher his own bird. Preparing my Sunday supper is a habit in which I take singular pleasure, a responsibility the women give me gladly. I sit through the last half hour of service tapping the hatters' plush of my topper in anticipation of scraping pin feathers. And then home, where sweet Julia has laid out my chambray and apron, where the women have scrubbed and prepared the bucket and stool behind the kitchen and placed a cigar and a short bottle of rye by the fresh-killed bird. The weather is crisp and warming. The women of the White

House kitchen grumble that it does not befit my station, but they learn that with power comes the ability to choose one's own path.

The idea for my Sunday ritual was Julia's. She knew I missed the pleasures of war and felt muddled in my new position. One night, she had a memorable dream in which I was severing the feet from a fat hen. In the dream, the hen's yellow claws pinched a scroll upon which were written the words ULYSSES GRANT, THE FINEST PRESIDENT. On waking, she rushed to my chamber and sat shivering at the foot of the bed while she told the tale. Her right eye crossed handsomely whenever her spirit was roused, and at that moment was so askew it appeared as if one eye watched the antechamber for an intruder as the other fixed upon me. I was reminded of the day I first met her, after service, her arms laden with stemmed dandelion flowers she had pulled from a patch beside the road. I said How do you do, and an errant bee stung her sweet armflesh and she dropped the weeds, screeching, wild eyes skewed, a devil woman before me, and I knew I would make her mine.

What measures can a man take to ensure control over his own experience? It was a question I often pondered on behalf of the soldiers under my watch. On behalf of them, to be clear, because they themselves were so filthy in the fields of Vicksburg and Appomattox that it was as if the sludge had entered their brains through the ears. I would treat them to fried oysters for breakfast and fresh coffee without the cut of chicory. We were all easily pleased in those days, and though there was no liquor I count that time among the happiest of my life.

I cut my cigar with the beak knife and twist off the bird's head. Its crop follows, stuffed with feed, and the gizzard, which I baptize with a splash of rye. The neck is reserved for broth. The oil gland slides free with a flick of the blade. I sing old battle songs while I work: one of a vacant chair by the fireside, another of the glory of emancipation. The viscera fall from the slit pouch, my empty bottle is replaced. The bird's heart, the size of my thumb, is reserved for the cats.

Satisfied with the process, I alert the women to the pile and take my leave to dress for supper. The window from my chamber affords a view of the new trees propped up with gardener's stakes on the lawn. I drag over a chair and enjoy a fresh glass as the sun shines over my property, my territory, my nation. By the time the meal arrives, the bird and I barely recognize each other.

Monument

The townspeople met at the graveyard at the agreed-upon time. They brought bottles of vinegar for the weeds and pails of water and rags and soaps. A gardener hauled in a truck bed of hardy plants, one lady had flowers tucked in a laundry basket, and a few of the men brought shovels to even out the earth around the yard's only tree. Someone started up a lawnmower.

Without much conversation, they got to work. They scrubbed gravestones until the names gleamed. The lawnmower sputtered to life and its owner began to trace the site's perimeter. A man gathered faded silk flowers in a trash bag. The children held smaller pails and cups of water and cleaned out the stones' grooved details with their fingers.

Each person gave their unspoken thoughts of respect to the graves they cleaned. These were the resting places of their friends and neighbors. Even those long dead had left generations in witness. Most worked in silence. An old man took a break from cleaning his wife's stone to wipe his eyes with a handkerchief. Someone whistled a hymn.

Work around the tree was going well. Its roots had disturbed the ground and the area needed to be smoothed and resodded. An usher at the church swung a shovel full of peat a little farther back than he had intended. The shovel clipped a gravestone and sent a piece of the stone flying into the high grass.

The sound rang out across the field, a light metal *ping*, and stopped the crowd. People looked to see what happened. A few dropped their things and came closer. Wiping their foreheads on their sleeves, they regarded the stone.

It was the grave of an upstanding member of the community, a woman who had been well loved when she died. Most of her kin were in attendance, and her young grandchildren played a spirited game of hide-and-seek around the graves. The man who had swung the shovel looked at each of them in turn.

The woman's eldest son stepped forward to inspect the damage. He ran his finger along the stone at its sheared point. The granite wasn't very old, but its surface had dulled after years of rain and sun. His mother's name was still clearly marked, and the grooves were rimmed with grime. A line of earth clung where the shovel had struck, and the stone that chipped off had given way to the mica sparkling inside. He laid an open palm on the place. The split portion, cool and freshly exposed to the afternoon sun, seemed tender to the touch.

When he lifted his shovel, the crowd took a step back. He swung it like an ax onto the gravestone, landing heavy and breaking off a larger piece. He leaned forward and touched the place again. It was so fresh it looked wet, as if a vein of springwater spread through it. Again he lifted the shovel.

The townspeople stood, watching the man's destructive work. After a few minutes, one of the women leaned down and put her full weight against a brittle stone. It fell, splitting cleanly in two, and she covered it with fistfuls of earth. An old man took a shovel to his sister's memorial, lopping off the delicate angel's head that crowned it. He scrambled after the head, scooped it up, and threw it with surprising strength over the far fence.

The crowd sprang to action. Children gouged limestone with their trowels. Someone went back to his truck for a baseball bat. A woman beat her husband's stone with her fists until she was pulled away and given a pickax. They worked in this way until nothing remained.

Two

Western Passage

I knew that man was trouble. He hefted a duffel above his shoulder without seeming to register its size, rubbing his body across each seat he passed. The people behind him had to stop and set down their things, waiting for him to finish fondling the headrests. He was dressed like a young guy but had the white pocked skin of a man nearing middle age. When he smiled at me, I held my gaze one inch into his eyes, not at but in, where he might register my personal wall. This trick took thirty years to master. From there, we had an understanding.

"Hey baby," he said to the girl beside me.

She ignored him, fussing with an exposed bra strap.

A silver chain strained his neck and another one, linked flat, held steady on his big wrist. Shaved hair stubbled his arms. His nails were groomed and perfect save for the one on his left index, which was missing, the naked nailbed pink as a cat's tongue.

He repositioned his bag. "You have a great smile," he said. He smelled like a fresh meatball sub. "Has anyone ever told you that?"

"No," the girl said.

"Who made you so beautiful, though? Did heaven make you that way?"

She turned to the window but her smile was visible in the reflection. Outside, a woman barred from the boarding area lay facedown on the sidewalk and screamed.

The man kept on down the aisle and the girl exhaled sharply through her nose.

I closed the book I was reading and held it on my lap. "That guy's a loser," I said.

She turned to see where he had found a seat. "I don't know anybody in Long Beach."

"He doesn't want to be your friend."

"He was nice to me."

The bus swayed gently as if we had rolled into a shallow pond and become buoyant. We would be going for the rest of the day, with one meal and two smoke breaks. I picked my book up again.

The girl sat with her back to our shared armrest, frowning as the scenery greened. "Do you think he likes me?" she asked after a while.

"I'm sure he does." I was reading a story about children with special powers. Their friend had become lost in the forest and when the other two went to find him, they learned of their own nuanced powers of sensation: the girl felt heat in the earth and knew that creatures were nearby, and the boy saw through dense trees and found a congregation of wild animals meeting on the horizon. The children walked bravely toward the beasts, holding hands.

"Do I look okay?" She looked in her compact mirror and handed it to me like it might still hold her reflection.

I caught the sour smell of her palms, which she had licked before smoothing her hair. "You look good."

With every step the children took, their bravery waned until it was like a tightrope under them. They shivered on the line but kept moving forward, sensing the importance of the gathering of animals.

"Really, tell me."

I held my page. She was skinny in cutoff shorts. Her polo shirt, likely designed for a child, was snug and ripe under her pits. Her hair was limp as if it had been taped on. Concealer caked around her lips, tinting her blemishes orange, while mascara gave her lashes the look of suspension-bridge cables.

"It doesn't matter how you look," I said. "His goal is to take advantage of you, with or without your consent, and he will not be your friend when it's over. You have to protect yourself from these men."

I went back to reading, satisfied that I had stopped an advancing storm. The girl sniffed her displeasure and traced patterns in the seatback. "I know what I'm doing," she said.

She accepted the cigarette he offered on the shady side of the McDonald's. They talked about the weather and how the back of the bus smelled like garbage wrapped in wet garbage. He told her she looked like a movie star, but he couldn't figure out who exactly.

"You need to watch it," I said.

"I'm watching everything," he said, smiling, so close to my face that I could have pressed my cheek to his.

"Me too," I said. "Everything."

"Come on," the girl said.

The driver called us to go but the man didn't break his gaze.

"Old bitch," he said in a convivial way.

"Not another word."

He put his hands up in mocking assent. His half-stripped finger bulged.

She was at me before I sat down. "Jesus Christ," she said, drawing it out.

"Trust me," I said. "I've been where you are now."

"I thought he was gonna kill you." We were rolling

out of Quartzsite. The man had found a new seat behind the driver and was clapping his big hand convivially on the back of a teenage boy.

"Attention is the most worthless currency on the planet," I said. "When you treat it like it's precious, you're blinding yourself to the possibility that you might find it elsewhere. And it's everywhere, attention is. You're a beautiful girl. You have fine features and kind eyes and a good line to your body. See, and now you're acting like nobody's ever complimented you before."

"Well," she said.

"I'm saying you may as well assign a high value to yourself. You should consider all the angles. His attention is a penny placed on a monument. Give the monument your prayers, not the coin."

She pressed her lips together. Her every movement came off like a minor miracle, as it was with young women. I tried to remember myself at her age, but when I tried, I only saw a girl lost in the woods.

"Do you know what I mean?" I asked. Watching her think about it gave me a thrill. It was nice to have an interested third party. I wanted to say more but stopped myself and allowed her to flatter me with her consideration. Outside, the landscape began to bear fruit. We trundled past long lines of orchards and roadside stands. I opened my book to return to the gathering of animals dancing in unison.

"What are you reading?"

"It's a story about magical children."

"Magical," she said, confused. "It's a kids' book?"

"Since you ask, I do feel more calm when I'm reading stories written for young people."

"Okay," she said. "I guess I don't get it."

"You certainly don't have to get it."

We rolled on. "You know," she said, "I just figured he'd want to hang out."

"Don't you have anyone to stay with?"

"My dad's out there," she said. "In Lakewood I think. I don't know."

"What don't you know?"

"I don't know." She rubbed her eye with the back of her hand.

"You should have somewhere to stay."

"That's exactly why I was talking to that guy if you didn't get the hint." A portion of her mascara had decamped to make a wet halo around her right eye. "He seemed fine and you ruined everything."

I tried to imagine what a benevolent character would do in my book. "You should stay with me," I said. "You need somewhere safe."

"With you?" She lifted one delicate corner of her lip. I could see her watching television on her belly in my living room, picking marshmallows from a box of cereal.

"Sure," I said. "For a few nights. Get on those feet."

She laughed. "No, I don't know. We'll see," she said. "You totally ruined everything else, so you owe me."

"You're right, I owe you." Without thinking, I reached for her face. Holding her chin, I wiped away the smudged makeup with my thumb. The girl allowed the movement, keeping very still and looking away. I cleaned her off, thinking about the vast system of payments and debts.

My apartment was just as I had left it. The sheets, stretched over the mattress on the floor, blended into the white carpet and bare white walls to lend a clean, institutional feel to the whole. The kitchen area, demarcated from the other space only by a change in flooring and flanked by white laminate countertops, was functional and airless. Taken all together, the place was immaculate—one room, but room enough for me. I plugged the television in and opened the windows. It was comforting to remember that I could keep a complete inventory of my items in such a small space. My books were stacked high in all four corners, with more on the card table. I moistened a paper towel and wiped dust from the counters.

She stood by the door, slouched under her two backpacks. Instead of carrying one on each arm, she wore one on her back and the second strapped to her chest, the overstuffed pack resting on her belly. They had a counterbalancing effect, holding her upright and steady under their equal weight.

"Take a load off. Want some water?"

"If you don't have any beer," she said awkwardly, as if

she had read about people saying such things but had never tried it out until now. I had to remind myself that I hadn't coerced her into following me, that she had gone willingly with me to the cab and into my home without so much as noting the street names.

I took two glasses from the cabinet and rinsed them out before filling them from the tap. "Put your things anywhere."

Leaning, she let her arms fall forward. The pack slipped off her chest and hit the floor hard. She righted herself and deposited the second behind her in the same manner, almost going down with it. "It's nice to stand," she said.

"Dusty in here," I said, more to the dust than to her.

"How long have you been away?" she asked, sniffing the glass of tap water I gave her. It was unclear to me if she was detecting odors in the water or the glass itself.

"Sorry, no ice."

We drank our water in silence. There was something metallic about it, though I may have invented the flavor to understand what she was feeling. Empathy, I found, was a good and valuable skill and I tried to practice it at least once a day. While we drank, I glanced down to see if her name might be printed on her bag. She craned her neck to observe the junk mail piled by the door.

"I'm only around here half the year," I said, sweeping the mail from the counter and dumping it in the trash. "Otherwise I'm in Texas with my brother."

"Your brother's in Texas." She seemed very tired all of a sudden.

"That's right. The state and I take turns caring for him."

"What do you do?" she asked. "Out here, I mean."

"I read and go to movies, and take classes at the community center. Business typing, supply chain dynamics, things like that."

Her eyes were lidded to the point that it seemed possible she was asleep on her feet. "Cool," she said. "Cool."

"Do you want to lie down?"

"I don't want to take up any space." She had edged herself into a corner and crossed her arms before her as if to prove her point, the empty glass pressed against her upper arm. She looked at the bed, placed in the center of the room like a low altar.

"Go on. I'll leave you alone."

I rinsed out her glass in the sink. She was asleep before she got horizontal. I nudged her bags into a pile next to the door and went to clean up.

The bathroom was as I left it, with its tinctures lined up in the cabinet. I chose two of the little bottles for later.

The shower sputtered rusty. The human stink of the bus had gotten into my skin and hair, the inner folds of my nose and ears. I could sense it seeping into my bloodstream. I had become the bodily equivalent of a pair of wet jeans. It was fine that she was ruining my sheets. I considered the alternative: allowing that monster on the bus to take her away, to fingerbang her in the back of some Camaro he called home. The water drove welts into my skin but I couldn't force it deep enough, even when I tugged my earlobes down, when I opened wide and sent it down my throat. The bus had left the kind of stain that coiled around my animal cells. Removing it would require weeks of pure living. I would have to throw out the sheets.

My brother and I were the kind of children who could spend an afternoon entertained by games of our own invention. We played Orphan and Soldier, shouting across the backyard. Or Leaf Lottery, where the winner could create the rules for the rest of the hour, maybe that berries were to become our only food or that we weren't allowed to call for help. He was ten years older and my only protector. Sometimes he wouldn't come home for a few days at a time, no easy task in the country. He must have made a camp somewhere.

Once, he was gone for a week when they sent me out after him. Stickers snagged my tights. It must have been Sunday and it must have been cold. I looked for him behind the shed and by the big oak, up the stream past the flat bank, past where we had ever gone together. I shouted his name, throwing sticks so the animals would be scared away. I took off my shoes, which pinched, and let the rocks cut into my stocking feet. I sat down and waited for an hour or two after I forgot if he was lost or if we both were or if it was only me.

Branches cracked and fell and the sound froze me toward their source. The sun had just set and shapes changed in the new dark. I bit down hard on my thumb, which I hadn't realized I'd been sucking.

He emerged from the forest, which settled back behind him like a curtain. He was naked to the waist despite the cold and was thinner than usual, his skin seeming loose on his body like a paper bag covering a pear. He asked me why I was scared. The air around me was the same as the air inside my body.

He kneeled on the ground and made a cradle from his arms. We had played Child and Cradle before. I curled up and his legs made a bough under my back. His arms were as cold as any branch. "Before we grew hair and got dangerous, we were all babies," he said. "Did you know?"

"Yes," I lied; I could only think of my brother as a fully formed man, even then when he was young. I knew already that he would send our mother away at last so that it could just be the two of us. The scope of our shared future was too much. His hands were hands and my body was a nursing doll.

She was running in her sleep. Her legs twitched. When I lay down, she instinctively rolled closer. I considered the possibility that she was dreaming of the man on the bus and the thought filled me with a flashing trill of grief and rage. I had saved her from him and she didn't yet understand how grateful she should be for my actions. I pictured her bloody in an alley, her gut ripped with a shard of glass; or perhaps she would be scattered across a public park in parts, oozing like a bisected worm. I thought of her hair tied to a buoy, a gleam of white bone from her open throat catching a fisherman's eye. But here she was, whole within her reliable container.

I edged closer and she cuddled up. Her lips planted on the skin stretched between my armpit and breast. I was naked from the shower. She pretended to be asleep for a while, and then her eyes opened and she looked over my shoulder to the wall. I estimated her to be one hundred ten pounds. After a while, I extracted myself and got up to make dinner.

"Do you like tomato soup?" I asked from the kitchen. "I'll have to make it with water."

There was no response save for her quiet cough.

"Tomato?" I asked. "Or chicken and stars?"

She sat with her back to me.

"Here's what we'll eat if we have chicken and stars," I said, examining the label, spinning one of the tinctures on the counter as I read aloud. "Chicken stock, enriched macaroni product, including wheat flour, egg white solids, niacin, ferrous sulfate, thiamine mononitrate, riboflavin, folic acid." Her silence met me; she might as well have slapped the food out of my hands. Such cruelty in such an otherwise lovely girl. "Do you hear me? Cooked chicken meat," I said, louder. "Carrots, modified wheat starch, lower sodium natural sea salt, chicken fat, celery, cooked mechanically separated chicken, monosodium glutamate. Salt. Sugar. Maltodextrin, onions, corn oil, yeast extract."

I sat beside her on the bed, ran my hand roughly through her hair. "You need to eat," I said. She didn't move. She wasn't disturbed by my nudity, by anything about me. It was as if we had known each other for a very long time indeed, our whole lives, or maybe our lives began in that moment, and either way she gazed clear-eyed into my heart and forgave me for all my future sins.

"Modified food starch," I said more gently. "Spice extract, cornstarch, beta carotene, soy protein isolate, sodium phosphate, and chicken flavor, which contains chicken powder." I squeezed her and put my lips to her shoulder. "It's important to realize all of the angles," I said.

She let me lead her to the table and sat while I made the preparations for her meal. "Table for one," I said. We were going to have such a time together and learn so much. Lucky girls like her didn't have the capacity to be truly grateful and so I felt grateful on her behalf.

The Death of James

There was nothing wrong with him, really. She watched him snoring there on the old couch his parents had given them as a wedding gift, a sleeping bag half swaddled around his big body. He was a good husband who listened to her stories from the grocery store, where she worked behind the customer service desk and had to deal with the guys from the bus stop bringing in lottery tickets they unwedged from the trash, changing the numbers, insisting they were real winners. Jim's thumb rested in his open mouth, a bad habit he had long tried to break with hypnosis tapes.

A good man. He would hold her face in his hands and say the sweet things. He spoke of soothing topics like yard maintenance, the work he did with pine bark and fish compost. He hadn't saved the violets the neighbor kids had trampled but figured the bare patches brought some realism to the scene. It would be properly summative to say there was nothing wrong with him. There were certainly things wrong with her, the blood pooling into her slipper suggested. The layer of tendinous muscle in her belly curled back to reveal a scroll detailing exactly what had gone awry in her own personal history. It fell from her and unfurled, inked script declaring ills: the time she overhanded a pair of bronzed baby shoes at the neighbor's dog; the time her boss found a tray of refill razors in her purse.

She bent over her sleeping man, feeling the intentions of her heart suspended in ego like a kitchen sponge in dishwater. Gathering up her nightgown, she tucked her knee under his. The penknife snapped a few seams in the couch frame as she hefted up beside him, holding his shoulder to keep herself aloft. He moaned, turning and settling back. He must have been such an easy child.

The disposal was stopped up. It had begun to produce an odor, which she had noticed earlier that evening while making his sandwich for the next day and considering the ways Miracle Whip could truly be called a miracle. She had rolled up her sleeve and plunged her hand to the blade, discovering it dull enough to mangle a lemon half without destroying it. Or else it was a problem with the motor, something prohibitively expensive. Either way, it held the fruit to rot, drowned and steady against her scrabbling hand and then the knife, yielding to the slight attack. She didn't have the strength or skill to fix it. There was so much that was out of her control.

A Gentleman

Angie was in the road, leaning against the curb. She had kicked her feet like a child until one of her crummy ballet slippers tumbled into the street, where it was run over by a bicycle. "I wish I had a dog boner," she said.

Mason made a noncommittal sound. He got down beside her. She was crouched between two parked cars, her arms all cut up. He reached for her chair to roll it closer but it was just past the grasp of his free hand.

"We are good friends," Mason said.

"To better express my feelings," she said. He could feel

the scars through her thick tights like seams on a fabric doll. Her legs made a graceful arc, ankles as delicate as a fossil of an ancient sea creature, like her body progressed back in time from head to foot.

"It's late."

He grasped one of her wrists and held it gently. She thrashed and kicked up a soaked piece of cardboard. "I wish I was a dog boner," she said.

"We should go home."

"I don't want to," she said.

"Your girlfriends said I should take you home."

She made a choking laugh. He was trying to heft her body onto his lap but only managed to pull her torso halfway over his knees.

"It's true," she called out. She reached for one of the cars, hooked her fingers around the bumper, and pulled. Her fingernails came back dirty. She smudged them across her face.

Mason appreciated the independent spirit that soared above her condition. Always since they had met he imagined standing beside her on a television program, maybe with his hand on her shoulder in a public show of pride and support.

She was vomiting. He turned her body to the side so she could avoid her dress. His hand grazed her breast and he moved it away, down to her belly because he was a gentleman. "We need to go home," he said.

Someone stopped above them, a man and a child. "We're fine," Mason said toward the man's knee. The child put its foot in the vomit and Mason placed his palm on the child's face and pushed it off. They went away.

"If I was a dog boner I would be vanished," Angie said.

"It's past our bedtime." He pressed his hand against the side of her head.

She produced a high growling noise. He saw her jaw working. He shushed her and she shushed immediately, which made him feel good.

"Cookies," she said, after a while.

"Let's go."

She moaned. Her bare feet looked cold and he closed his hand around one to warm her. He thought of himself as a gentleman.

Away From

He showed me a bottle and said he could use some company. I figured I could use some, too, and so I went, as he was my neighbor and we had common ground between us, I mean underfoot. Think about all the times you ever wanted to rest. He was my neighbor and I saw him around every now and then walking. We went to his house and picked up lighters from the corner store on the way. He didn't seem that strong at the time.

His house was big and there was a grill on the porch. In Vegas we were all trying to stay low to the ground like lizards, but here, houses can be three floors. There was a lady sitting on the couch and, not being friends or strangers, I said Hey, and she gave me this look and I said All right. And then going up the stairs he put his arm around me and said Honey, hey honey? We walked together like that, like I was his old girlfriend.

Quick as that, we were alone. We smoked and kissed some; he seemed very strong all of a sudden. He tied my hands together above my head with a power cord and got my shorts off, watching me the whole time, my face. He said he was preparing to kill me and there wasn't anyone who would notice, not during and not after, since he was right there by Ted's, and he had a point, Ted's being a place that sells meat.

I thought to myself Well now you are in a predicament. I decided to act as if this was a normal thing and we loved each other very much. I would have held him gently if I had use of my hands, but I did not and so talked of the weather, which had been fine that morning. Once he was finished he started crying and talking about the things that made him do it, for example a girl he was dating and the drug. He was trying to understand something and I realized if he figured it out, this might change things in a way I was not prepared to handle. I suggested we rest a little and work things out later. He fell asleep right away, which I found stranger than anything.

My child and I lived in Vegas for two years in a house I rented from a lady I found online. She left the keys for us in the mailbox. It was a little place with one bed and a busted wall unit but the price was right. I would sit with my back to the window open to the windless night and watch my child while she slept. She had my full attention in those days. We walked through the places on the strip, never stopping for anything, just to get out of the heat, holding hands like I was taking her to the bathroom. She was five or six then and has since been taken from me by the state. She liked the gardens at the Flamingo and I read the plaque they put up there for Bugsy Siegel while she ran around. The thing about Bugsy Siegel was that he was a gangster and a white man. I read up on him while I waited. When the bank took the house we had to leave and I never did meet the lady who owned it.

This all occurred to me as the room showed itself like it was rising from a sea. First it was me and the man and the bare walls, and then I saw we were on a mattress, and then the clutter of paper sacks from Ted's and old clothes. There were five pairs of women's shoes lined up under the window. All this washed over me. There in the man's house on his mattress on the floor it got in my head that if I left his side—his arm draped over me, the cord wrapped round my wrists above my head—if I even breathed too deep, there would be a psychic energy disturbed and he would know. My gut had carried me this far, I mean through my life, and also through the day's events, and I did notice there was an open window in case he blocked the door. My arms went numb and I slept soon after by some magic brought on by stillness. When we woke up later I asked as natural as anything if he could untie my hands because I had to go pee, and he did like from a dream and went back to sleep.

In the bathroom I noticed the mirror and sink were very clean, but there was stuff jammed up under the bowl like maybe rust stopped with wadded-up paper. It reminded me of a time a boy in school bust his lip in the lunch line and it bled through a cloth. I figured it was time to go.

I didn't want to flush because then he'd rouse from bed and expect me back, but I didn't even want my pee standing in that place and so I flushed to ensure it would flow out through the pipes and find a river. My shorts and shoes were gone but I knew it was important to leave right then and I could ask the woman downstairs for a towel to cover myself. I could already see the back of her head from where I stood on the stairs. I took one step and the next but the third creaked and his hand clamped over my mouth.

I tried to think of when my luck had changed. It was maybe when I got off the bus and saw him sitting there, watching it roll on, and my brain said That one right there. It pointed, my brain: That one. Right there. The thing about drugs is you can fight them all your life but you're fighting a brain that wants you dead, and the thing about fighting is you can't fight forever. The thing about Bugsy Siegel is that his room at the Flamingo had one way in and five ways out. Anyway, he dragged me back.

Fifty Ways to Eat Your Lover

When he buys you a drink, plunge a knife into his nose and carve out a piece.

When he asks you what you do for a living, dig into his spine with a broken juice glass.

When he wonders aloud if you ever get that feeling about someone, bite his tongue out of his mouth.

When he says you have a beautiful body, seize his Achilles tendon.

When he slides his hand under your thigh, sliver off his earlobe.

When he persuades you to spend the night, sink your teeth into his collarbone.

When he asks if you're on the Pill, squeeze your pelvic floor until his penis pops off.

When he wakes up in the morning, clip his eyelashes and snort them.

When he makes the bed, open up the vein inside his elbow.

When he stops by your place after work, crush his skull with a tire iron and lick his brain.

When he gives you a book he likes, dip him into a deep fryer.

When he asks you out again, stab him with a box cutter and suck the wound.

When he wants to know what movie you'd like to see, wrap a piano wire around his testes until they drop into your mouth.

When he takes a picture of you, grind his toes with a pestle.

When he asks where you've been all his life, clamp your mouth to his side-meat.

When he asks you if you're going to write about him, push a corkscrew into his shin and chew what curls out.

When he takes you to meet his parents, smother him with a pillow and eat his middle finger.

When he moves his books into your apartment, take a grater to his knuckles.

FIFTY WAYS TO EAT YOUR LOVER

When he brings home a puppy, shave the skin from his heels.

When he tells you he loves you, paper-cut his fingertips and suck their blood.

When he asks you to marry him, panfry his foreskin.

When he takes you to Paris, wrench his wrist and gobble the tendon.

When he builds you a desk, tap a piece of bone from his hip with an awl.

When he asks you to get off the floor, wedge an oyster knife behind his kneecap until there's space in there for your tongue.

When he works late and won't discuss it, peel off a layer of his facial dermis.

When he slams the door, spread citric acid across his nipples and latch on.

When he kisses someone else, flay his abdominal skin.

When he says he's sorry, snatch his nose.

When he tells you that you don't love him, rip a fistful of hair from his head and put it on your cereal.

When he wants to know if he's made himself clear, press your thumb against his eye socket and slurp the goop.

When he says he's sorry you feel that way, peel off his toenails and sprinkle them on a salad.

When he says he needs some time off, jam his hand into a toaster.

When he shows up with flowers, nibble the hair from his arms.

When he invites you on a walk, crush his elbow in a vise.

When he asks if you'll take him back, tuck your fingers under his lowest rib and pull.

When he draws you a bath, sever his smallest toe.

When he offers you his arm, squash his neckflesh in your fist.

When he asks you to wear the dress he likes, slice off a slab of his buttock and serve it to yourself on a plate.

When he wants to know if you think he'd be a good father, broil his viscera.

When he marvels at how much time has passed, gnaw the skin between his fingers.

When he asks you to take it down a notch at the Christmas party, pour wine into his ear and drink what drains out.

When he teaches your kids to drive, masticate his chin.

When he takes you out for your anniversary, squeeze his forearm until it bursts.

When he says you've looked a little pale this year, open his throat with a rough wedge.

When he drives you to the doctor, cut a knot of muscle from his upper thigh with a handsaw.

When he sits with you for months, chew off the tip of his thumb.

When he tells the hospice nurse to leave you both alone, work a tube into his larynx.

When he says you've had a good life together, force your finger into his mouth and scrape out his soft palate.

When he says he'll miss you, dig a spoon into his belly button.

When he says goodbye, eat his heart out.

The Moment of Conception

We wanted a child so badly! Even then, when she suggested the procedure, I wasn't sure about it at first. It didn't seem natural.

She pointed out that the fact we hadn't made a child, when we both wanted it so much that we each dreamed about it every night, was not very natural, either.

It was true. My nightly dream featured a wide, dark field lined with bowing branches, a line of dogs running ahead of me in a single-file line. Their feet would pound the earth and I would feel an earnest and magnetic connection to them, my body being pulled along behind.

Meanwhile, she often dreamed that she was walking through a hallway of carriages filled with sand. She would wake crying if she had a chance to touch the sand, which she described as being very cold.

We were sitting up in bed together, sharing a bowl of chocolate pudding in the nude when she spoke of her plan. Neither of us much wanted sleep. We had made a life together, a quiet house. In the center of our home was our bedroom, and in the center of our bedroom was an extravagant bed, which we had specially made. The mattress was out of reach from the floor and getting in required scaling one of two ladders mounted to either side. We would take our meals there.

She dipped her spoon into the pudding and licked it off. She said, I've been thinking about this for a long time.

It would be nice if you would alert me when you were thinking of things like this, I said.

I have the supplies ready, she said. She told me she had read about certain creatures in the ocean who experience this phenomenon naturally.

You might as well show me the supplies, I said.

Getting down onto her naked belly, she scooted toward the stepladder. She was always a handsome woman and had only grown more so with the sprouting of wiry gray hairs, each reminding me of a sensitive antenna tuned to the stars. I recently discovered a gray, almost white hair jutting proudly out of her mons pubis. The other hairs seemed to show it some deference, curling below.

She padded to her closet and returned with a shoebox. She placed it at the foot of the bed, out of reach, before mounting the stepladder. At the top, she got on her belly again and scrambled up, rolling toward the center of the bed and patting the mussed sheets around her. She pushed the box over to me. Inside were sewing needles curved like half-moons, thick coiled thread, a hunting knife, and a vial of white powder atop a folded plastic sheet.

You found my knife, I said.

This would mean something to me, she said. And what's more, she said, I think this really might work. She was coaxing me into tumescence through the sheet. I held her hand still with both of my own.

It involves some sacrifice for the both of us, she said. She removed her hand from my grasp and took the plastic sheet from the box, unfolding and spreading it over the comforter. She lay down on the plastic and gestured toward me.

A few items made an appearance in my head in quick succession, dominated by the thought that it was difficult to find a person with whom I shared so many of my hobbies and habits and that if I left her, our dual presence would be missed on the court by our badminton league for months to come. But it was more than that; this was a woman who gave up a job in the city to be with me. She made a pastry for us to enjoy each Sunday, featuring food items of individual or mutual significance to us. There was the lemon cake for my years in the seminary, the chocolate ganache for one of her long illnesses. I knew from her kindness and her spinach torte that she was my spiritual equal.

Thinking of her value, I entered her easily and we held there for a moment, looking into each other's eyes while she readied her hand. She touched my hip, kissed my neck. When I was positioned properly inside her, she grasped the base of my member with a firm hand and sliced it off, the knife's clean cut blinding me as if it had severed my optical nerve as well. I collapsed to the side and felt pressure from her hands holding something to my body, a cloth, and upon regaining my vision, saw her injecting herself with a compound, and upon waking some time later, saw her sewing her bloody sex closed, my own still inside, with a hooked suture needle, a look on her face of such steady concentration that she seemed to express a controlled rage, and I saw that my body was already closed and cleaned and healing under a fresh linen bandage.

We woke much later, pale and thirsty, the plastic sheet sticking wetly to our bodies. Her breathing stuttered as she moved her head in the crook of my arm and then she was quiet. There were things that we would do for each other, sacrifices we would make, and the proof of that fact was before us as plain as an hour in the day. It was a beautiful morning or afternoon.

Journey's End

Once you counted eleven hundred days, you lost the desire to count. You threw out your notebooks, which freed up some space for fuel. Those days we were looking either for fuel or for places to store it. We opened every closed space, every fridge and trunk, every clotted gallon jug, finding mostly rot and the occasional mummified corpse of something small like a squirrel, which either had tried to hide itself or had found its end at the hands of others. I began to fantasize what might happen if we discovered glowing cubes and cracked them open to find blistering stuff of the universe within. I didn't miss you counting the days like you needed a record. Like any authorities picking us up would want to know the details of our survival. I figured things would be better when you gave all that up and I was right.

We found fuel in plastic bottles and tins, some mixed in with orange juice. I would have almost rather had the juice. There was one double-zip bag of fuel and one of vinegar that used to be wine at the base of a pile. I found a cooler of urine buoying rotten cans, their metal bowed out, contents sunk in a haze at the bottom. Some industrious individuals filled every light fixture in an empty house with gasoline. We marveled; they had freed delicate glass from metal and filled each bulb, soldered to reattach, and affixed in place. If the power ever came back on the whole thing would go up. It wasn't clear why anyone did the things they did. You remembered your father obtaining a wood-boring drill-bit set; after he died, you found that every book in his house had been ventilated and the trees out back as well.

Behind the bulb house we found our third video-game cartridge, maybe the first that might actually work in a console. You saw it first, its black half-moon tucked under a pile of makeup tins, their pressed powder turned out beside like a fleshy pyramid. Our goal after some walking was to settle down, and such a cartridge was on our short list of essential items. We would find what we needed and once we got everything we would stop.

We settled that week in a nice place. There was a bed for us, the cellar was clean. Someone had semiprofessionally engraved his family crest into the door. There was an old set and console. I hooked up the generator and didn't immediately die. You blew on the cartridge and snapped it in. We held each other when the old familiar sound emerged. I wanted to break the screen and employ the services of its glass on my face but you warned me to be careful after all we had been through. You were thoughtful like that.

Three

These Are the Fables

We were in the parking lot of a Dunkin' Donuts in Beaumont when I told Kyle. I figured I'd rather be out under God as I announced the reason for all my illness and misery.

I said Well shit. Guess we're having a baby.

"Lemme see," Kyle said, frowning at the test for a second before tossing it into a planter. He flipped the double deuce to a stranger who had set his coffee down to applaud. "People these days," Kyle said.

I said my folks would be happy.

"Here's the thing though," he said. "Your folks are dead. And I have a warrant out for my arrest. And you're forty years old. And I am addicted to getting tattoos. And our air conditioner's broke. And you are drunk every day. And all I ever want to do is fight and go swimming. And I am addicted to keno. And you are just covered in hair. And I've never done a load of laundry in my life. And you are still technically married to my dealer. And I refuse to eat vegetables. And you can't sleep unless you're sleeping on the floor. And I am addicted to heroin. And honest to God, you got big tits but you make a shitty muse. And we are in Beaumont."

I said these were minor setbacks on the road to glory.

"And," he added, "the Dunkin' Donuts is on fire."

Indeed it was. Customers streamed from the doors, carrying wire baskets of bear claws, trucker hatfuls of sprinkled Munchkins. "Get out of here," one of the patrons said. "The damn thing is going up."

Listen, I said. We're going to have to make it work, we'll forge a life on our own and the child will lead us.

The wall of donuts had fueled a mighty grease fire. The cream-filled variety sizzled and popped. Each ignited those within proximity. Their baskets glowed and charred. The coffee machine melted. The smoke was blue and smelled like a dead bird. I popped the lid off Kyle's coffee cup and puked into it. All I had wanted that morning was an old-fashioned and the absence of puke. I said that everything would be all right, that we were living in the best of all possible Dunkin' Donuts parking lots.

He pushed some dirt over the test with the toe of his boot. "Poor thing," he said. Between his sensitive nose and sour stomach, we both knew the next nine months plus the eighteen to twenty-two years after that would wreak some manner of havoc. I put the coffee cup on the ground because the trash bin inside was consumed by flames.

He took my hand and we got out of there before the cops showed up to the fire and started checking IDs. He stopped at the Kroger and came out with half a dozen roses, which he laid between us on the dash.

"Let's get back to the Rio Grande," he said. I tipped my seat back and dug in to sleep while he took the tollway. The coast was speckled with cities with names that would suit the spines on a grandma's bookshelf. Sugar Land. Blessing. Point Comfort. Victoria.

We ended up at the Days Inn in Corpus. Kyle examined a road map in his underpants while I took the bucket to the ice machine. A crowd of tourists were standing in the laundry room. They were speaking languages.

A young woman touched my ice bucket. "We are looking for where Selena was murdered," she said.

I said I didn't know what she meant.

"Fifteen years ago at this very Days Inn," the woman said. "I am disappointed in you." An older woman was leaned up against the ice machine. She had her face pressed into her hands and her hands were pressed into the ice machine.

"They won't tell us where," the younger one said. "They changed the numbers on the doors so we won't find out." She pulled me close. "There are secrets at this Days Inn," she said.

I said that there were secrets at every Days Inn. The ice machine was broken and the women wailed for unrelated reasons.

"Our angel," one of them said. She was holding a gilt-framed photograph of Selena singing on stage. She did resemble an angel. I wanted to lie down on the laundry-room floor.

In the room, Kyle was eating a waffle the shape of Texas and reading the syrup packet. I stood in the open doorway.

"The first ingredient is corn syrup," he said. He was a shadow in the back of the long room in his buttoned shirt and a clean pair of pants. He had his shaving kit out on the table. The blade was drying and his face was shorn and cold. He said, "The second ingredient is high-fructose corn syrup."

I told him he looked like he was preparing for a funeral.

They say that hotel-room floors have *E. coli* but I lay down anyway. Kyle came and settled near me. When he pressed his cheek against my belly I could feel the machine motion of his jaw grinding tooth on tooth. I said These are the fables we will tell our child.

Gutshot

The man was gutshot. His blood welled around his hands and soaked his shirt. "I'm gutshot!" he said.

The man who had shot him lowered his weapon. "That is definitely what I intended to happen," he said, "but now that it's happened, I feel things have gone too far."

The gutshot man drove to a hospital. "Doctor, I'm gutshot!" the man said.

"This is terrible," the doctor said. "Wow. What are we going to do?"

"I hoped you would know."

"It has been many years since I practiced medicine. They let me stay here. Soon they will name a surgical ward after me, where men who are gutshot can be cared for."

The doctor drove them to the home where the gutshot man's mother lived. "Mother, I'm gutshot!" he cried.

"My sweetheart!" his mother said. "Woe descends upon us all!"

"I'm not sure it's as bad as all that," the man said.

"Upon the beginning and the last end, view only the comfort of darkness!"

"He seems to be pulling together," said the doctor, who had returned with a set of towels to stanch the blood.

"All ye who pass through these walls and halls will know only pain through the end of days! Please don't use the guest towels."

"We're going to go sit outside," the man said.

The doctor helped the man to a place behind the house where an elm tree made a bed of fallen leaves. "Good luck," the doctor said, climbing over a fence and running for the road.

"Jesus Christ, I'm gutshot," the man said.

"Well, now I won't help you," Jesus Christ said. He was seated on a low branch. The bottoms of his sandals gently brushed the man's forehead. "It speaks to a lack of respect, you know."

"Truly?"

"Just kidding. I love you. I also love the man who gutshot you and I love what you're doing to those guest towels."

"Will you help me?"

"Oh, sure. Do you see that airplane up there?"

Jesus Christ pointed until the man saw a silver glint in the sky.

"The people in that plane are flying to Dallas," Jesus Christ said. "There is an old woman who feeds the stray cats in her neighborhood, and a dentist, and a little baby who will grow up to be in asset management. There is a pilot who loves the smell of masking tape and a woman who doesn't know what she wants to do with her life and will eventually stop wondering."

"And they're all going to Dallas."

"Does that help?"

The man leaned against the tree trunk. His vision flared and blurred. "I think so," he said.

How He Felt

"I love this woman!" the man told the empty room. "What should I do to prove my love?"

He bought a billboard by the main road and ascended its ladder with a can of paint and a broad brush. But the board was much larger than he had figured from the ground, and he could only reach the lower third of it.

"I live this bath mat," a mother read for her child as they drove by.

The man had his message printed on a massive banner with the thought of flying it over the bay, but the pilot he hired was an inexperienced crop duster and a drunk, and he rigged the banner upside down and backward. People on the beach craned their necks to look. A pair of jet skis collided, killing three.

He rented a movie theater, but the reels were accidentally switched and his invited guests puzzled over a sex-education video from 1964. He composed a song and taught it to a children's choir, but they contracted food poisoning at a pizza party and spent the evening drinking Gatorade and playing video games. He wrote it into a sermon, but the pastor threw the whole thing out as sacrilege.

Discouraged, the man drove to the site of his billboard and ascended its ladder again. At the top, he held on to the platform as the panels groaned in the wind.

The man wanted to share. He knew that if they only understood, the population would be forever changed. He rested his head against the billboard. He heard in the protests of the steel a message from the mechanized world. He thought it was a love song, but he was mistaken.

Labyrinth

Dale had been doing a lot of reading on Hellenic myth, and so when he said he had a surprise for us at his Pumpkin Jamboree, we knew he wasn't screwing around. The Jamboree—a weekend he organizes on his property to bring the town together and raise a little money for the fire department—features a hayride, face painting, and a cake-walk occupying the side yard entire, but his corn maze tends to be the highlight.

A crew of hardcore maze-runners formed a line before he had even finished setting up. I deposited my five bucks like everyone else. "Only it isn't a maze this time," Dale said, arranging a last bale of hay around the pumpkins from the patch. "It's a labyrinth."

A general murmur rose. "What's the distinction?" asked a woman holding a whorl of candy floss.

"I'm glad you asked. It's largely the fact that the path is unicursal, not multicursal. There's only one road, and it leads to only one place."

"There's no point if you can't get lost," said a townie kid who was known for pulling girls into hidden corners of previous corn mazes and taking advantage of their confusion.

"Also," Dale said, "each of you has to go in alone."

"It's no fun alone," shouted a pretty girl who was implausibly holding the townie's hand.

"My kids aren't going in there by themselves," said the high-school football coach, taking a knee to clutch two boys to his chest.

Dale held the bucket back from folks reaching for their money. "Calm down," he said. "Nobody has to go if they'd rather not. To be clear, the labyrinth is known to possess magic. Some say that once you find the center, you discover the one thing you most desire in the world. Others claim that God sits beyond the last bend. Individuals must learn for themselves. Go check out the jam contest if you're not feeling up to it."

"There's no way," one of the firemen called out, a little drunk. The man was undoubtedly a guest of honor for the weekend and held some influence over the group, which began to turn away and head for the fest's other features. The rope pull was another favorite.

Dale watched them leave, fingering a pumpkin's thick stem and surely considering his hours of lost work. A few months beforehand, he cuts into the young corn when it's tall but not yet sprouted, taking a pass first with the tractor and then with the riding mower to pull out the brace roots and tamp it down. He does the maze plans on drafting paper and displays them in his swept-out garage addition—he calls it the Hall of History—with other jamboree memorabilia: the gearshift from the original hayride truck, trotter prints from the winning pigs. We gather around to remember which wrong turn we took and what was waiting on the other side.

Knowing what he put into it, I thought it was a shame to stand by and see everyone go. The sun was still low in the sky and it was lonely at home, where the TV had been broken for a week and the tap water had begun to taste oddly of blood. "I'll go first," I said. "I'll do it."

A few of the others stopped their exodus. The pretty girl—whose name, I remembered, was Connie—let loose of the townie's hand. Unfazed, he ambled off to do drugs behind the house.

"That's the spirit," Dale said. "Jim will do it, everyone. He'll start us off."

I shook my friend's hand. "I know you worked hard on this maze and I intend to take full advantage."

"It's a labyrinth, but thanks. That's the kind of brave

spirit we're known for around here." Dale made a point of looking at the coach, who was still on one knee. Shamed, the man stood.

"All right then," I said, and made to get started, but Dale stopped me. He dug in a bag at his feet to extract a piece of clay trivet, the type that allows a hot dish to sit on the dinner table.

"You'll need this," he said.

The trivet was etched with strange symbols. There were men and warriors and saws and a shield and something that resembled the buttock of a woman. I became keenly aware and deeply uncomfortable with the knowledge that the others were crowding around to observe the etchings, which were in my hands now, a fact that implied my consent. "I don't know about all this," I said, to clarify.

"It's the Phaistos Disk," Dale said. "I paid a pretty penny, so mind where you set it."

It did seem to be imbued with some significance.

"How'd you get that?" one of the women asked.

He waved her off. "Let's say I got lucky during a period of government oversight on the part of the Greeks. It puts a finishing touch on my project. Now you go on, Jim. This is my life's effort distilled. Find out what it's all about."

It was a few degrees cooler inside the labyrinth, which imparted a sense of magic though in truth it was only that the low sun was shaded by the corn. The soil smelled wet and new and the path was wide and curved slightly to the right. Following its progress proved the bend continued on thirty feet before coming to a switchback. The stalks didn't do much to block conversation on the other side of the wall, and it was possible to hear the others discussing the merits and folly of my decision.

"You remember what he did on the hayride last year," someone said. "Some asshole was screwing around and let his cigarette drop, started a fire in the hay right in front of a bunch of kids. Jim there took it upon himself to jump out of the truck and run for the fence. He wouldn't come back and so we put it out and went out looking for him and when we found him, when we found—" As always the tale involved some heavy laughter at this point.

"That's enough," said Dale.

"When we found him—"

"Oh my God," a woman said, preemptively, though at that point the story may have easily been finished in gesture. And so the shame of the fire found purchase once again. You could live your whole life in the smallest town and still find strangers to tell a story like that.

The trivet was a good weight, conducting my hands' heat. It was further comforting to trace the etched shapes, settling a fingernail in the arc of a scythe or buttock, which on closer inspection could just as easily have been a winding river, so simply it was carved.

Turning another switch, it became apparent I had lost some sense of place. The corn walls rustled. The voices faded and the only sound was the grouse pond on the far edge of Dale's property. On I walked, holding the trivet to my chest. I wasn't accustomed to carrying much of anything and so the disk's weight was fatiguing indeed. I made a sincere promise to start up again with my dumbbells in the garage.

The sun had begun to set and a cool breeze filtered through the leaves. After another switch and twenty paces, the voices returned.

"You've got to hand it to him for going in there alone," the man said, the same one who had told the terrible story. "Maybe he has that adventuring spirit after all."

The surprise I felt at this praise stopped me and I held my breath to listen, but there was no sound until I started up walking again.

"He's got balls," said Dale, a true friend.

"I never knew he was so brave," a woman said. I stopped again and waited longer this time, counting out the seconds and reaching a minute, then three minutes, five, hearing only silence as if they had all of them lost interest and left. I took a step in the direction I had come but it felt like pushing against a strong wind. The trivet was exhibiting a lateral weight as if it was magnetized to the far horizon. Still I labored against it. The pressure nearly tipped me on my rear, causing me to experience a devastating picture of myself emerging from the maze soaked down the back of my jeans, clocking in for another year of ridicule. And so I turned and continued into the labyrinth, at which point the conversation began again.

"I'm glad to know him," I heard Connie say.

It was a thrilling statement, but I knew better than to stop and try to hear more. The journey was providing an immediate reward, and though I was panting and making a heavy noise in my footfalls, the conversation seemed somehow amplified the closer I came to the center. Their voices provided sound's equivalent of a compass star in the dusking sky.

"He has a strong heart," a man said.

"I'm so proud of him," said Dale.

"Actually, I find him pretty handsome," added Connie.

Their voices buoyed me on, losing only slight volume when I was heading away from them, and I broke into a trot that carried me around the far side, taking the turns without pause, drawn all the while by the trivet, which seemed towed on a wire. "I wish he'd come out here so I could shake his hand," someone said wistfully, but there was no way to stop. The switches were coming faster and the path narrowed, as if Dale hadn't quite figured out the proportions required. Young leaves brushed my shoulders.

I didn't realize my exhaustion until, turning the last corner, I found the center. The moon shined a straight beam into the clearing, which was six feet wide, with a divot in the dirt the size of a man. The trivet was straining toward the ditch. It took my whole strength to hold it back and my strength was failing. But I had to keep it safe. Dale had given it to me with two hands, looking me in the eye.

With the last of my power, I turned to stand between

my burden and the pit. The trivet did its work from there, pushing me back and down, into the hole that seemed to have been dug to suit me, complete with a rise in the dirt for my neck and a uniform pile just below my feet. The trivet settled in the center of my sternum. It grew cold there and heavier than before, though I felt no desire to move from under its wind-removing weight. I saw now that it was a stone like any other. I found that once I stopped struggling and held very still, barely breathing against its mass, I could hear the crowd again. They were telling stories of my heroism and bravery, of underwater rescue and diplomacy—tales I couldn't remember being a part of, though surely I was involved in some way, if so many recalled them so fondly. Eventually I did try to stand, at which point I realized the trouble.

"Folks?" I said, quietly at first. "I think I got stuck on a root structure or something."

They continued their talk, even grander than before. Someone brought out a guitar and began to improvise songs which told my origin story. *Born to a rancher just a little west of here / Jim raised his head and never cowered out of fear*, went one line. My lungs struggled to fill against the weight of the stone.

"Dale?" I called out, gasping. "I need help. Can you bring a crowbar?" I was being driven down into the dirt as if by a machine press. The carved glyphs bit into my chest and branded my skin. I was alone. Then I met the Minotaur.

Device

The young inventor created a device that could predict the future within one-tenth of a percent of accuracy.

"Device," he said, "tell me the winner of this Saturday's football game with Tech."

"State wins," the device said. "A man will pour beer onto his jeans."

"Seems likely," he said, marking it. He thought of his girlfriend. "Tell me, will I marry Anne?"

"No," the device said. "Anne will move to Missouri.

You will find a similarly adequate mate. The colors associated with your wedding will be sea green and ivory."

The young inventor had been dating Anne for ten years. He took the news with the composure of a scientist and adjusted a knob on the device.

"Sea green and ivory," the device repeated. It sounded flat and bored, and the scientist made a note to swap out the vocalization for something a little more upbeat, perhaps accompanied by music.

"What will my eventual mate be like?" he asked, tweaking the machine's color wheel.

"Skin, hair." The device buzzed lightly. "Fingernails."

"Not too much specificity there."

The buzzing stopped. "Grass and milk."

"Will she be interested in science?"

Some process caused a turning over in the internal works of the device.

The inventor tapped the panel. "Will we be happy?" he asked. He could hear the whirring. "Device, will we be happy?"

The device was silent. After a while, the young inventor packed his things, collected his lunch bag from the refrigerator, and left.

The empty room had its own energy. "Algae and bone," said the device.

The Swan as Metaphor for Love

A swan's foot, like a duck's, is a webbed claw. In travers-
ing swan shit and mud, these claws naturally gunk up and
reek. Nobody in the history of the world, save another
swan, has licked a swan's foot while that foot was still attached to the swan. The feet resemble rabid bats in their
sickly color and texture.

Moving north on the swan's undercarriage, one will find
an eroded civilization of swan shit and pond scum. This is
a banal phrase, "pond scum," one that is easily ignored, but

look closer. Swans eat grasses, sedges, and pondweed, each teeming with murk. They will also eat insects, snails, and a fresh shrimp if they're near one.

Pond scum is more of the same: swan shit, fish shit, frog shit, half a can of beer poured by some fuck teenager, plastic, photosynthetic residue, algae, permanent bubble, hexagon patch freed from its soccer ball, arthropod corpse. All attached to the swan in its idiot float through its stagnant little inland sea.

Swans eat tadpoles. A swan will slurp up entire schools of larval amphibians, process them, and shit them out, and then sometimes it will sit in the shit or walk through it, and here we are. Anyone who claims that a swan is a majestic and noble creature has never seen a swan up close.

Swans will attack you if you are nearing their young or their nest, if you are trying to have a conversation with their mate. They have jagged points on their beaks, which resemble teeth but more closely resemble a plumber's saw, which plumbers call a Tiny Tim. If you try to take a swan's picture he will strike you with his beak. Too much attention enrages a swan. The swan has a long neck and will strike at you. The swan will bite you and tear your flesh.

Swans mate for life, which is maybe ten or fifteen years. Someone found a swan once that was twenty-four years old and probably it was mating for life, which everyone made a big deal out of even though the swan was not even old enough to rent a car. The swan wasn't yet acquainted with life enough to silently hyperventilate in its bed. The swan didn't have a bed. The swan was too stupid to have a bed and if it did it would fill the bed with swan shit.

That's all for today about swans.

Year of the Snake

They didn't think it would last all year. Ten months at the most. When the snake appeared as a broad green sunrise on the horizon it was January, an inhospitable month for snakes. But this was no ordinary snake. It crested the far range and barreled down the main road, flattening trees like wet reeds in its path. It towered over the farm mercantile and humbled the line of threshing machines. The townspeople ran from the square, but the snake settled and didn't move to coil around anyone, not even the smaller pets. It wedged silent between the south awning of the schoolhouse and the north entrance of the bank.

The snake stayed put for a few days before anyone approached. Naturally the first to gather the courage was Martha Swale, the town scientist. She walked to the outskirts of town and into an apple orchard, where the snake was resting its head on the limb of a sturdy Braeburn, its tongue snapping bark off the trees as it tasted the air. Swale propped up a ladder and climbed, pad and pen in hand, to take measurements of its venom ducts. The snake allowed Swale to span its eye sockets with her tape, heaving what the onlooking farmers described as a resigned sigh. Indeed, she found, the creature had the same proportions of a standard snake, only larger by an exponential degree.

Back in the town square, a team of engineers examined the damage done. The snake was so wide that the front façades of some of the buildings were thoroughly crushed. The creature had become load bearing where it was wedged under the schoolhouse's roof and against the bank's pillars, preventing their collapse. As long as the snake didn't move, the structural damage was not the type that threatened either building's integrity. One engineer patted the reptilian flank and remarked that the poor girl was stuck. Nobody questioned his determination of sex, as the engineers were perceived as simultaneously knowing everything and nothing at all.

Time passed, and the people grew bold. No apparent clues arose in the mystery of how the snake had come to be, or where, or why; as generations before had found, there was little utility to questioning the unknown. Children made one flank into a climbing wall by leaning boards against its body. Down the way, they used their bikes to section off a court for their handball games. The mothers stood by nervously, but when no harm came to their babies, they went on with their daily work.

Even Swale found herself more interested in the physical presence of the animal than in its origin. As with any bridgeless river, it was difficult to traverse the snake, and so the town was split in two. People started referring to landmarks and locations in terms of the new barrier; the school, church, and nicer homes were in North Snake, while the bank, movie theater, and poorer homes fell within South Snake. Children in South Snake couldn't get to school anymore, and instead played handball games all afternoon. The children formed rowdy gangs and roamed the area, knocking down mailboxes. In North Snake, people started spending more and more time in the church, until a group of a dozen or so individuals held a constant vigil there, praying all day and night at turns for the health of the snake and for the death of the snake.

A devastating insomnia settled over both sides. The snake's presence had thrown off the whole town's biological rhythm. People stayed up late, watching from their porches. They took shifts and acclimated to fewer hours of sleep. Nobody wanted to turn away in the event that it might continue its silent progress, or—God forbid—eat a child, though the snake hadn't budged in months and one had to travel into the orchard to even see its fangs. Still, nobody wanted to wake and find they had missed any major event, and so they slept less and less. Soon enough, everyone could stay awake for weeks at a time. Schoolteachers rubbed their eyes as the children before them multiplied and vanished, turned sepia-toned, and spoke in tongues. Butchers forgot to log deliveries and had to throw out pounds of spoiled meat.

Swale, who lived in a small apartment in South Snake, observed the darkening circles under the eyes of her neighbors. She suffered a very bad haircut from a woman who paused during the experience to lean against the wall and weep. Watching the woman slide down the wall, Swale realized there was a need. Though she was born and raised to research and she made quite a good scientist, she also aspired to invent and produce a product. Her mother had inspired this dream when she made the very good point that since Swale was unemployed with neither prospects nor money, she would soon have to move back in with her parents—and she didn't want that, did she? She did not. And so, one afternoon, she brought her kit to the snake.

Children played handball around her as she worked. First, she took a rubbing of the scales and examined their feathery tips on a page of contact paper. She pressed a sponge into its side to see if a liquid might emerge, and then swabbed the area with a moistened cotton ball. Neither technique successfully disclosed any material, and she tapped the snake's side with her fingertips, considering it. She went to her kit and returned with a fine razor.

Working slowly, she shaved off the tip of a single scale. The reptilian wall shifted with discomfort while she made her incision but calmed once she applied pressure. She examined the sample—a silvery aqueous thing—and used an even finer razor to cut a slight piece, as thin as an eyelash. A gentle titration of the slice in a saline solution caused the material to change slightly, producing a blue glow that matched her calculations. She added another shaved piece to find the solution glowed even brighter, a pinpoint of light in the waning day. The vial's contents produced a gas, popping out the cork. It glowed with an organic heat. She detected the slight odor of cloves. This was precisely what she had anticipated. Like any good inventor, Swale tried the potion on herself, downing it in one go. It tasted like a rubber ball. She held two fingers to her lips, burped, and slipped to the ground, unconscious.

She woke surrounded by curious townspeople, the night sky at their backs. Her head had been propped up awkwardly against the snake. She rubbed her neck and patted the ground for her pocketwatch. Six hours had passed. And there it was: a sleeping potion to rival any drug, easily administered and instantly effective. And what was truly interesting, she saw once she stood to examine it, was that the snake's scale had completed its regeneration process. It was impossible to find the spot where she had taken her sample.

The potion worked so efficiently that each individual required only one glowing drop. Folks quickly learned that they should be in bed at the time of dosage, as its immediate effect had them wreaking accidental havoc, smashing into stacks of books and pulling down tablecloths. One woman woke to find herself wrapped up in a load of wet laundry she had tried to hang before the drug kicked in. A man banged his forehead on the side of his drafting desk on the way down and gave his wife quite the scare.

People put in bulk orders. A half-drop formulation worked with children and a double drop treated the obese. The streets cleared out at night. Someone tossed a small package of the drug over to North Snake with usage instructions. Eight hours later, a baseball wrapped in cash came back with a note reading MORE OF IT.

A new empire rested in Swale's hands. She hired a pair of assistants, taking only a pin drop of her own treatment and waking a few hours later to get back to work. She shaved thicker pieces from the snake. Her young assistants mixed the solution and marked their observations. Swale stood at the sentient wall with her hands on her hips, regarding her vast potential fortune. For all she knew, the snake didn't mind the knife. The faster they cut, the faster the scales regenerated.

There, in the heat of production, wary Swale heeded the kind of impulse she typically wouldn't follow. It was a caprice inspired by growing demand, distinguished only by its thrilling mixture of success and greed. In that wild moment, she pushed one of the assistants aside and plunged her surgical steel deep into the snake's flesh. The blade sunk as if being pulled by a new gravity and then was sucked from her grasp. She found herself elbow-deep in the snake before she thought to draw back.

A cracked line of light crowded from the wound, and with it a suffusion of warmth. Swale stared as the snakeskin parted and smoked, peeling back to reveal that the flesh inside formed a cavern. She saw a lantern swinging gently from the knobby spine ceiling. A man sat at a table, regarding her, as calm as the moon. The man turned Swale's surgical steel in his hand. He resembled a laborer of some type, perhaps a farmer. His long trousers were dark and he was barefoot. An old cap drooped around his eyes, which squinted at the intrusion.

"Hullo there," the man said. "Please, come in."

Swale stooped as she entered the cavern. Behind her, the townspeople gathered, each silently convinced that they were experiencing a hallucinatory side effect of the sleeping drug.

The man sat at the table and gestured for her to join him. The lantern played shadows on their faces. The air felt cold and pure, like inside the case at a flower shop. The man lit his pipe and leaned back.

"I'm sorry to disturb you," Swale said. She took in the room. "How do you survive?"

The man shrugged. "I was minding my own when this big girl rolled up and swallowed me whole. Fortunately she took a few provisions with her as well. It's not so bad, really."

A sound like the rustling of wet paper drew Swale's attention toward the townspeople. The snake's skin had begun to regenerate, stitching together and closing the gap. She saw one of the engineers reach out tentatively and draw back.

"I ought to go," Swale said.

"You might stay for dinner." The farmer dug into a box at his feet and pulled out a tin of trout, placing it between them like a jewel. He pulled on the hair at the back of his neck as he watched for her response. He seemed kind, really, and she hadn't eaten in some days. The sound of the townspeople ceased as the scales sealed up around them.

"All right, then," Swale said.

The snake began its slow progress out of town. The monumental shifting motion, a silent quaking of the earth, set the dogs to howling. The bank walls trembled and the schoolhouse awning crashed to the earth. On the outskirts, the orchard men woke from their drugged sleep to find the snake had taken out a series of apple trees before it found the road. Its tail lashed against the church, crushing the façade and leaving a trail of glowing scales like fireflies in the young night. It was only then, after the hazard was gone, that the people of the town saw the deep divide it had carved between them.

The Heart

I think it's a whale's heart. I saw one in science class on a video, and I asked Miss Prichard if there was any kind of animal bigger than a whale and she said there was nothing bigger than a blue whale, so I figure that's what it is, a blue whale's heart, here in the living room, as wide as a car. One of the kids at school says You would be cool if you weren't so stupid, and I think like Yeah, this heart is the same way. We came downstairs one morning and there it was, and Dad said whatever kind of heart it was, we needed to get rid of it.

These days when I get home from school, I get into the drawer in the kitchen, where our three knives wait in a shoebox lid. The knife he chose for me has a thin blade and I've got a good technique on it now. I take up one of the buckets and head for the living room.

My brother pretty much only gets a knife so he can feel like he's helping. Me and Dad would get to work—Dad and I—and then Applebee would cry, even when Dad told him that boys in kindergarten do not cry. So we gave him a butter knife and told him to go for it. It calmed him down, and though he isn't making much headway and doesn't really need a bucket at all, he is happy and so we are happy, the three of us, working on the heart. Dad tells stories about hunting and describes different techniques of cleaning animals, which he says he used to do more of, like maybe every month.

Slicing into it gets worse every afternoon. In the first few days it was really bleeding and smelled like the trash behind the grocery store, which is to say not good, but then it dried up and the smell went away or maybe we got used to it. Then it got rubbery, and it was like cutting into a milk jug, and even Dad was having trouble and he had the big hunting knife that he once used on bucks. Sometimes he would be going at it and he would say Damn it, and then we would all kind of stop and he would say Sorry. He says it's there because of Mom and I figure when we get it cut down enough she'll be inside or at least we'll get some clue about how to find her.

Dad rinses out Applebee's lunch box and we take up our work without too much talk. He passes us our knives handle-side out, for safety, though it's worth mentioning again that there is no way my brother can hurt anything or even himself. He would do more damage with a spoon, but he seems happy, so whatever. It's good to work without having to talk about school. Nobody really cares what Applebee made in Crafternoon and he seems to be okay with that.

I have figured out a technique against the heart where I glide the knife in sideways like I'm cutting a fish open. I do this a few times and then there's a dipped bit where Dad can come in and peel off the chunk that's too high for me to reach.

We slice and drop. Once a bucket is full, we take it to the can behind the house and try to not make a big production about it if there's a neighbor looking.

The heart is cold and dry on the outside but grows warmer the more we cut into it. It seeps a little onto the carpet, not blood but something else, thicker. As it heats up, it starts to really stink like a pile of dead centipedes after rain. Dad and I tie bandannas around our faces and I try to help Applebee put his on, too, but he's a baby about it, which is totally expected, and then he steps in the stuff on the carpet and tries to walk into the kitchen and Dad tells him to not track a mess and then he cries for a while and Dad and I just stand there, staring at the heart in front of us, with these bandannas on like we're wild hunters, like we're waiting for a massive buck to walk into the living room and allow us to climb on from the couch and then carry us on his back over the horizon line and I say that I miss my mom and Dad says Sure.

I take Applebee upstairs and help him wash his feet in the tub. There aren't any clean towels, so I dry him off with my shirtsleeve and then he gets his jams on and I tuck him in and turn off the light and he cries a little more and I sit with him for a while in the dark. My hands smell like a dead whale basically. As he's going to sleep I'm sitting there and feeling tired out from the work, and I feel stupid for wanting to go to sleep without watching any TV, but the heart is kind of blocking it. Applebee sleeps finally and I sneak out of his room and head halfway down the stairs to tell Dad that I'm going to bed, but he's down there working on the thing still and kind of singing to himself and I figure I'll leave him alone.

A Contest

The gods decided that, once a year, they would have a weeklong contest and allow the one person who felt the most grief over the loss of a loved one to have that loved one return. They made a contest of it for their own curiosity and amusement and to boost morale in the beyond. It was a hit on the planet: Piles of flowers obscured the names on every cemetery grave and highway shrines glowed elaborate with electric light. A wealthy man held a parade for his mother, which spanned eight city blocks and included great rolling floats representing her spinach casserole and childhood home. On a flat expanse of farmland, a woman used sweaters and slacks to spell out ALAN in the event the gods passed overhead in a helicopter, as they sometimes did. Three girls scrubbed the grime from the corners of their friend's locker and decorated it with streamers. Somebody's grandfather placed a single rose on the pillow beside him and wept until he died, thoroughly missing the point. A child's preserved room was filled with candy until the windows broke, spilling wrapped butterscotch and strawberry suckers into the street. Weeks later, on the third floor of an apartment building, a woman opened her door and saw that her little black cat had found his way home.

Go for It and Raise Hell

The sun beats the shit out of a dirty road called Raton Pass where the closest thing to a pair of matching earrings is a guy named Carl who punches you in the head with his fist. There's a car on this dirty road and the car is as dirty as the road itself. It could vanish into the road because it is badass camouflage, but this car refuses to vanish. The driver of the car has taken it off-road and is spinning the shit out of its wheels, flipping endless bitches in this ugly desert.

This is the literal goddamn opposite of two middle-aged people going on their first date in a coffee shop. If this dirty car spinning its shit is on one side of the world, the opposite side of the world is a coffee shop where a fifty-three-year-old woman named Dolly describes the clay pots and saucers she is fixing in her greenhouse. Carl is not aware that there exist fifteen different kinds of peppers and three different kinds of lettuce. If he has in fact seen a basil plant, he called it a fagweed for the benefit of no one but himself, doused it in kerosene, and lit it on fire. He watched it burn and felt deeply satisfied.

Carl is the operator of this filthy camouflaged vehicle flipping endless J-turns just off this dirty shit Raton Pass stretch of road. The car is a Chevy Camaro IROC-Z from the year 1986. Carl puts nineteen dollars and eighty-six cents of premium in the tank and orders the cashier to keep the remainder of a twenty. It is the only kindness Carl affords. He leaves exact change for his breakfast in town. Waitresses don't dare say to his face the shit they say behind his back. These waitresses have heard of basil, but they are wary.

Say one word against Carl's Chevy Camaro IROC-Z and Carl will kill you. If you are scared that there is nothing you can be sure of in this world, you can be sure of that.

Carl has lived a hard and terrifying life. He draws great pleasure from fucking a waitress named Dolly in Raton, where the closest thing to a motel room is a janitor's closet with a door that locks. People who say that the desert is God's land and it should be protected are not referring to the city of Raton. The best thing to do out there is to spin your tires and curse every injustice in your own language as you grip the wheel of a Chevy Camaro IROC-Z crafted during or after the year 1986.

This car is spinning its shit into the hot earth, chewing up cactus spike, scattering wild creature. Carl is not wondering what happens if the cops come down and see the demolished twelve littered in the backseat. He does not think, Who can I trust to share my secret thoughts? Carl's thinking that if this was the opening scene of a movie he would call it GO FOR IT AND RAISE HELL.

Carl is coated in the filth of the world. Carl does not believe that the meek shall inherit. He knows that you never know what is enough until you find out what is more than enough.

If you asked Carl what the point of it all was he would spit into a cold cup of coffee and say Handjobs. After he left, Dolly would pocket his exact change and shake her head, but she wouldn't say a thing because she knows that if there is any man in this world who can impregnate a woman by raising his voice, it is Carl.

There is a Carl on the other side of the world. This other Carl might put on a black button-down shirt, with sleeves, and go out with a woman who talked about what it was like to grow fifteen different kinds of peppers. He might observe this woman while she applied lip balm and wonder in his lizard brain if she had the kind of meaty ass you get when you stand all day every day. His name might also be Carl, but he would drive a pre-owned Honda and feel like a pussy all the time.

Carl imagines the first minutes of GO FOR IT AND RAISE HELL. Dolly's there, except she has these stacked fake titties, and she's wearing this silver bikini that shows off her Grade-A Prime. In the movie she's sitting in the passenger seat of the Chevy Camaro IROC-Z as Carl flips these righteous bitches. She is speaking but it's too loud to hear her and too dirty to see her dirty mouth.

Dolly knows that the way to a man's heart is through his vice. She knows how to make it count. Slowly she is speaking, and speaking slowly she is saying GO FOR IT AND RAISE HELL.

Dolly and Carl on the other side of the world would get married. Dolly would wear a wedding gown that held her body like a fat man sliding down a mountain, and Carl would duct-tape tin cans to his Civic. But here in Raton, they're doing just fine. Here, the road of excess leads to the palace of wisdom, and that road is paved with handjobs.

The Lives of Ghosts

Marcy noticed the pimple when she came home from the hospice center. She dropped her bags, her mother's bags, and the plastic tub containing her mother's jewelry and saw it right away, examining herself in the hall mirror. It had risen overnight. It stretched her cheek's skin with a soreness that assured Marcy it would surface and disfigure just in time for June's wedding that weekend. She produced a tube of benzoyl peroxide and dabbed it on before going to bed.

It was even worse in the morning, warm to the touch.

Marcy frowned, her bleary eyes struggling to adjust to the morning light.

Over the sound of the faucet, she heard her mother's voice: DON'T TOUCH IT.

She froze. "Mom?"

The woman's voice came again from the spot on her skin. YOU'RE JUST GOING TO MAKE IT WORSE.

Prodding the pimple, she felt her mother's presence. "Mom," she said. "Listen. I'm so sorry. I meant to get to you sooner. There was a flight delay, and you know how those are, and when I asked the attendant—"

QUIT FUSSING, her mother said. YOU'LL BE LATE FOR WORK

She dropped her hand.

One of her coworkers had left a condolence gift of a small potted plant in a mug by her keyboard. Marcy took it with her into the bathroom. She craned her neck in the mirror.

WHAT DID I SAY.

She jumped back. "Jesus Christ."

JESUS WON'T HELP YOU NOW.

"Of all the places you could end up, really."

The pimple was silent. She jabbed at it with a wad of paper towels.

WATCH IT, MISSY.

"This is a big week, you know, I have stuff to do. June

picked me as her maid of honor after all. You remember June. There are going to be pictures."

OH, IT'S GOING TO BE SO MUCH FUN.

Another woman came in and entered one of the stalls. Marcy applied lipstick while she waited for the woman to finish, but it quickly became clear that the woman was going to wait Marcy out, and so she took the potted plant and decamped to the breakroom.

"This comes at an exceptionally bad time," Marcy said.

TELL ME ABOUT IT. I WAS ABOUT TO PAVE THE GARDEN.

She dumped the plant out in the breakroom trash and filled the mug with coffee. "Couldn't you possess something at my place? That slow cooker you gave me would be fun to haunt." She bought a candy bar from the machine. "I've got some red shoes you could make dance whenever I wear them. We could do a road show."

I DON'T APPRECIATE YOUR ATTITUDE.

"I'm trying to talk some sense into the situation."

YOU KNOW, THAT CHOCOLATE'S JUST GOING TO MAKE YOU BREAK OUT.

"I can't take a meeting looking like this."

AND FORGET ABOUT YOUR FIGURE.

A man looked up from a nearby cubicle. Marcy ducked behind the wall. "I'm going to spray someone with pus in the middle of a sentence," she said, keeping her voice down and holding her hand over her mouth for good measure.

I'LL TRY TO CONTAIN MYSELF.

"I highly doubt that," Marcy said, though in truth her mother did seem subcutaneous in the way that could ache for weeks without coming to a head.

Tucking half of the candy bar in her desk for later, she organized her tasks for the morning. She would have an early lunch with June, who would know what to do.

"Everything is ruined," June said. They liked to meet at a sit-down Mexican place between their two office parks. The pimple counseled Marcy to order an iced tea and a salad, which she stabbed at obstinately. June was eating a tomato sandwich that she had brought from home. "I'm making a huge mistake."

"You're having completely normal thoughts. You're an intelligent woman and right now you're simply considering all the angles."

She crumpled the wax paper from her sandwich and stuffed it in her purse. "I appreciate that. I just think it's too late."

"You know you love Dave. You both deserve happiness."

"He's a good man," she said. "I'm probably cursing myself. Hey, get a load of that monster on your face."

Marcy hovered her hand over the pimple as if to shield it. "That's my mom."

JOYOUS NUPTIALS, said the pimple.

"Thanks a million," said June.

The waiter refilled their water glasses and silently regarded the sandwich June had left on the tablecloth.

"She's been here all day," Marcy said, after he left.

"Check this out," June said, leaning back in her chair. She lifted up her shirt a few inches to reveal a swollen spot on her belly. "It's Eric," she said. Her old boyfriend had been killed by a dog on a morning walk some years ago. "He's telling me I shouldn't do it." She rubbed her stomach tenderly. "He won't shut up. He talks all night sometimes. I don't know why I don't get him cut out of there."

BECAUSE YOU RESPECT THE DEAD, Mom said. June shrugged.

The waiter returned. "May I take your crust?" he asked.

"Fuck off," June said.

YOUR FRIEND IS RIGHT, Mom said later, in the car. SHE SHOULDN'T MARRY THAT MAN.

"She's a little hung up on Eric, is all. She gets that way. I once had to tell some strangers in a movie theater that her husband died in a war."

The pimple vibrated slightly and grew a small whitehead. ENERGY DOESN'T DIE, it said. TOO BAD FOR ALL OF YOU, RIGHT.

"Calm down," she said, starting the car and cranking the air-conditioning.

COME ON, YOU'LL BE LATE FOR WORK.

She focused on her breathing. "I miss you," she said. "I really do."

I KNOW, BABY.

The redness eased slightly.

"I miss you so very much," she said.

HEARD YOU THE FIRST TIME.

June was a happy, if pale, bride, wincing at the effort of walking on her father's arm. She wore a satin shift which had the unfortunate effect of playing up the swelling and giving her a sickly pregnant look. People whispered to one another as she passed them in the aisle.

The photographer's assistant had tried to cover Marcy's pimple with a concealer before the ceremony, but Marcy waved her off. It would shine as if it contained its own light.

The wedding party gathered to watch the first dance. Dave bowed to June and she took his outstretched hand. They danced to something slow, cheek to cheek. They made a handsome couple. Old men held their wives in the crowd. They got halfway through a slow turn when June fell.

The crowd reached for her, but nobody moved to break the circle they had made to watch the dance. Dave kneeled down to his bride, who was clutching her stomach, but she clawed at him and he reeled back, calling for a doctor. Her legs splayed like a doll. A pink stain was spreading across the silk of her gown over her stomach, darkening to red, drenching the fabric. She howled like a creature.

THAT POOR BOY, said the pimple. LET'S GET OUT OF HERE.

Marcy ran to her car and tore out of the lot, throwing her heels into the passenger seat. She thought of the desperate look on her friend's face. Stopping at a diner on the way home, she walked in barefoot and ordered a milkshake, fries, a slice of peach pie, chicken tenders, and a patty melt. The food arrived all at once and she pressed every course to her cheek, grinding each in turn until, over dessert, she was asked to leave.

Christmas House

Christmas House is an interactive, inclusive holiday residence. It is home to a manger scene, a gift exchange, a holly-hanging sing-along, and standards of the Yuletide such as hot buttered rum and various nogs. Visitors to Christmas House are charmed to see such traditions carried out in the spirit Jesus Himself might have intended, had He been a businessman.

Christmas House is a truly participatory experience. If a guest wishes to behave as if he or she is the first in the world to discover the act of becoming profoundly drunk on warm nog, that is his or her right. If a cast member wishes to tear down the mistletoe and declare that no man will ever understand true sorrow, he or she should act on that motivation.

Christmas House is home to fifty-three poinsettias. One cast member's sole duty is to distribute these poinsettias in an efficient manner while maintaining the spirit of Christmas. The cast member must bring together everyone he or she knows, apologize for being a burden, and award guests one poinsettia each. After their departure, the cast member must remove the leaves of the single remaining poinsettia, place them in a blender with warm water, and create a vitamin-rich paste for his or her face and neck.

Christmas House never sleeps. The first shift runs from dawn until dusk, the second from dusk until dawn. Cast members must remain within Christmas House during business hours. Cots and beds can be found upstairs. Infants employed by Christmas House may sleep during their manger shifts.

Christmas House sits at the far end of a firing range. At times, a bullet may shatter a window and nestle into an opposing wall. Cast members decorating windows must manipulate the sashes with boughs and hanging garlands while keeping their bodies tucked aside. The manger is bulletproof and hidden from the public.

Christmas House is not responsible for injury. If a guest is caught by a stray round, he or she must be carried to a location off-site and allowed to seek medical attention independent of the operations of Christmas House. Cast members are permitted to treat wounds in the spirit of Christmas, for example by compressing a blood-soaked trouser with holly leaves while singing "Silent Night."

In accordance with the true spirit of Christmas, guests and cast members of Christmas House must balance illusion and truth. The tinsel is penance and the figgy pudding is suffering. The Yule log offers no reprieve. Carols are sung, but nothing that rhymes is true. The hidden manger is in operation at all times. Individuals doubting the mystery of the season will be escorted from the premises.

Four

Viscera

After Exercises in Style *by Raymond Queneau*

This page was once plant material, crushed and sluiced and pressed through a machine in a warehouse, the process overseen by a man plagued with a skin infection. The man, ankles swollen after the sixth hour on the job, would loosen his damp shoelaces for some late-day relief—the flesh pillowing over his yellowed athletic sock—and would scratch the pimpled back of his hand, his wrist, and his arm so liberally that a steady snow of flaked skin would drift onto the pages as they flew through the pressing machine. Naturally the pages, which told the story of an uneventful journey, became infected with his particulate matter. His wounds wept in the morning but after a hot afternoon in the warehouse had almost fully clotted, carrying their weep in scab. Continuing his factory tour, the man found such perverse relief in rubbing a particularly affected spot on his forearm that his eyes rolled wetly back and his mouth dropped wide, allowing a line of spittle to gather at his lip, roll down his chin and over his stubble, and drop onto a speeding page bearing the climax of another story immediately before its entrance into the oven, baking the genetic evidence of his future heart disease into this very page, which you are touching with your hands and which will find its way into a used bookstore, perhaps after your own death from heart disease, where it will be touched by people ill with the flu, sinus infections, the kind of solid stuff that moves out of the body like a bus pulling out of a station, the empty seat waiting.

Date Night

The woman and man are on a date. It is a date! The woman rubs a lipstick print off her water glass. The man turns his butter knife over and over and over and over and over. Everyone has to pee. What's the deal with dates! The man excuses himself. At the table, the woman scratches her forearm a little too hard and a slice of skin peels up with her fingernail. She tries to smooth it back but it doesn't go even when she presses her palm to it. It curls around itself like a pencil shaving. The woman is dismayed.

She holds her hands on her lap when the man returns from the bathroom. He pulls back his chair and sits heavily. When the woman sees him, she covers her mouth to stop her laughter. The man must have washed his face too hard in the sink, because his left eye and cheekbone are stretching apart. Bits of paper towel are stuck to his cheek. He has wiped off his face! He observes her mirth with a skewed sullen glare until she shows him the skin of her forearm; then, he laughs with her. He uses his butter knife to scrape up a portion of his own arm to match hers. She plucks at her cheekbone until it forms a sharp point. He grasps his thumb and twists it hard. It pops into his palm and he overhands it into the kitchen. The woman bares her breasts and flicks her nipples off her body like flies on a summer day. They land on the floor and a waiter catches one under his heel and slips across the tile.

The other patrons have been watching this central pair. Underneath the couple's skin a clear paneling emerges: a carapace, a subcutaneous shell. Their bodies are mannequins carrying skin and clothing and color.

A wild look enters all eyes. Individuals wipe flesh off one another with napkins soaked in wine. A mother gnaws her child in its booster seat. One man lifts his ruddy toupee to reveal a few pathetic strands of glue-coated hair, blond in color, which he swipes off in one motion and stuffs down his shirtfront. Another man flicks open his button fly.

His pubic hair scatters like dandelion florets. The man howls and a woman rips his dick off and drops it into a bowl of soup. What's the deal with soup!

Tablecloths are pulled from tables and the tables themselves are scrubbed of their color. A waiter dumps a tray of meat onto the floor, shines the tray on his ass, and wears it as a breastplate to go into battle with the cook, a stout man with a blistered face. The cook uses the dishwasher's rags to wipe himself clean, revealing a featureless figure dripping with rage and shame. He tips a boiling pot of pasta water onto the waiter, who himself is freed from ears, hair, dermis, and his white waiter's gloves, a pair he had once bleached every night and which now gunk up the kitchen drain along with a holiday ham and a full set of teeth.

The room contracts. A woman screams until someone slips a dessert spoon under a muscle in her neck and flings her larynx to the floor, at which point the woman grasps both breasts, rips them from her body, and applies them to her throat. The breasts produce twinned howling wails that consume a grown man whole. Flesh is siphoned into a bowl and poured without discrimination into a free-standing grandfather clock that is set on fire and rolled into the street.

There rises a rallying cry of mutual recognition. This is no blind agony. It is a celebration! Every piece of internal armor on each individual is so thick with shine that even light from the recent past and future finds a way to burst forth, shattering across shattering glass, covering all in a blinding healing bleeding screaming LIGHT because that's what LIFE is, you assholes! That's what it means to be alive!

Curses

Our mother has become the object of our curses. The first was a rash made to climb up her arm like a creeping vine. She saw it when she was cleaning a breakfast dish and set down the soap to idly scratch.

"What in the fine hell," she said. It was a poor curse and performed in a hurry. If she had consulted the proper sources, she could have stopped it all right then. Blessedly, she is the type of woman to slap a bandage on a runny rash should it start to crack and bleed, the type to ignore a heart murmur on the occasion of her child's birthday. She would hope to die on an Easter weekend so as to reuse the church lilies.

The second curse happened soon after, when each fingernail on both her hands began to darken and smell of scorched plastic. She scrubbed them with acetone. Layers of nail commenced flaking off into shaved-looking piles.

"It must be that dish soap," she said. We nodded. At night we curled under blankets and carved incantations into our shared palm. We each had our own hand, but it was the one that joined us that made us special.

She yelled from her room in the morning and we rushed in to find her hair gone from the top of her head. Her lovely yellow hair, which she would brush and plait each night, was clumped on the pillow like a cat beside her.

That was enough. She told Phillip to get the car keys and drive us to the urgent care. We sure did, looking like a funny family on the Classic's front bench, fiddling with the radio station while she sobbed, nails black as a boar, clutching her hair in a bag on her lap as evidence for the ladies in the clinic.

We had to wait an hour and a half among the others in the waiting room. They breathed in unison and the room expanded and contracted like a lung. One man had cut himself open with a thin blade and another looked ill from drink, while a woman next to him ate a hamburger from the top down, savoring the bun's upper half before licking the mayonnaise from its toasted bread. The tin shutters on the windows bowed inward as everyone inhaled. Mother was plumbing the depths of her bagged hair like she'd find a jewel therein. We set immediately to a spell.

It was a nasty set of tricks to play, but truly she chose her destiny throughout. The curse we sent arrived in the form of a line of ants marching in from the swinging glass door and heading for her ankle like they smelled honey under her skin. We watched them shrink as they approached her, to pinpoints and smaller, so small that she wouldn't feel them when they sped over sneaker and bunched sock onto her bare skin, finding individual hairs and pushing into her pores.

She felt them soon enough. We imagined it was like sensing her blood was moving independent of bodily whim, which must have felt ticklish in an unsettling interior way. She reached over and clutched Morris so hard that we squealed. The ladies at the clinic were acquainted with dramatics but they weren't prepared for Mother's violent dance. One of them came around the counter and restrained her with both hands. The women looked into one another's eyes and Mother started crying out of pure shame.

The woman gathered her up and said, "You twinsies follow us." It was rude of her to deny us our intricacy, and in response we caused a small blaze among the paperwork on her desk. The fire was large enough to startle the desk staff and waste a pitcher of water. We were thrilled at our new and exciting control.

We were brought to a checkup room and the woman went back to attend to the mess on her desk. Without delay a doctor arrived and ignored Mother in favor of examining the stretched web of baby skin connecting our arms to the shared hand. "I've heard about you," he said, smiling at us. This pleased us immensely and we saw to it that his dinner that night would be delicious. Morris nuzzled the doctor's hand.

Mother gripped the table, her blood surely writhing. We started to feel a little bad about it, but there was nothing to do but wait until the ants shrank to a cellular level. They would remain, their antennae a swaying villi mass in her small intestine, but she might not be so discomforted. The doctor was asking us about how we dressed and slept and Phillip was explaining the shared seats and tailored shirts while she thrashed.

"Remove these demons," she cried, terribly hoarse.

The doctor glanced at her file and put it down. "I'm not sure how to begin," he said, producing an otoscope to examine our ears. "Your record notes a rash and hair loss, but I wouldn't jump to any conclusion that involves a demon or demons."

"These boys—" she said, before Morris touched her with a gentle hand and removed her ability to speak. She jabbed at us, and we focused our thoughts until the blackness on her nail spread. Finger and nail dropped onto the floor like a crust of bread. The sick spread from her finger to her arm and she watched it, weeping in pantomime. The doctor began testing our reflexes with a rubber mallet and marveling at the transference of reflex.

"I wonder sometimes what it would be like to have a sons," the kind doctor said. We laughed and laughed!

Blood

Your boyfriend's dad taught us how to explode mosquitoes. All you needed to do, he explained, was flex your arm and some mechanism would lock the insect to expand until it burst. Your boyfriend's dad was a contractor who worked on places in the neighborhood and lived on a street lined with unfinished homes. He said that all we've got is our minds and our muscle and so we ought to know how to use both. He would jab at your arm and say Isn't that right, Joshua? And you would laugh and rub the back of your neck and agree that he was right.

The neighborhood was the type where all the houses went up at once, so fast that their wood all surely came from the same trees, sheetrock from the same stone. You let me tag along with you and your boyfriend and sometimes he gave me ten dollars to get us some cheeseburgers.

We tried the thing with the mosquitoes for months, skipping the sprays and creams that might ward them off. We never saw them get us. We were pocked with welts that stung under tanning oil. I remember running across unfinished rooftops, jumping from house to house, but that wasn't right. It was your boyfriend's dad who did that and only once, striding a gap onto a garage extension to avoid climbing down and climbing back up. He was strong and cocksure, and seemed fairly confident in his own immortality. I'm still attracted to any man who can whistle.

Your boyfriend was all right. He played the violin. The three of us were lying on a roof once and he said that after death your consciousness snaps out and that's all. I thought he had fallen asleep. You said that when you died you wanted your ashes cast into marbles and distributed to your family. I would get the one that looked most like a galaxy, and your boyfriend would get the second. If anyone died, you said, it wouldn't be one of us. He shrugged and said it didn't matter either way. We climbed down and looked at the beams where one of the guys had drawn maybe one thousand separate pairs of tits. I was reading a book in school about a girl who folded paper cranes and so this made sense.

The three of us rode our bikes to the community pool and watched the girls playing tennis. I always found three or four spokey dokes for my bike in the playground by the court, the plastic nibs half buried like they had grown there. We once broke a ramp constructed at the base of a hill for our red wagon and that was the worst thing that happened to any of us, as far as I knew or cared. The idea that everything was fine laid the delicate foundation of my life.

You figured out the mosquito trick right at the end of the summer, before you went to high school and I stayed with the little kids. It was the sweet spot of August and almost my birthday. We were sitting in a half-finished house at the time, drawing in the wood dust on the concrete, when you called my name and I saw it was stuck in your arm, at the prime point of your bicep, placid and feeding, swelling like a tick. Once it burst we shouted with joy. We spread its mess around with our fingers. Afterward I would wonder why the mosquito didn't fight harder against your skin, why it didn't strain to free itself, if it maybe knew how special you were.

Precious Katherine

The doctor chewed on his lower lip as he worked. "That explains it," he said.

Mark and the doctor looked into the metal pan together, in which a lump of bloody tissue rested, plain as the afternoon and free from Mark's anesthetized shoulder.

"I don't see it," Mark said.

"There it is."

They leaned in close. The tissue was perforated by white flecks and a ribbon of darker stuff.

"There's a nearly functional endocrine system here."

The doctor ticked up a tag of flesh. "Explains your mood swings. There's a little heart, right there. And look," he said, coming away with one of the white flecks balanced on his blade. He held it up to the light.

"A tooth," Mark said.

The doctor clapped him on the back. "After all that, a goddammed resorption. Never thought I'd see one outside a book." He gave the pan a gentle shake, revealing a rib cage as delicate as a bird's.

"Can I keep it?" Mark asked.

"Her," said the doctor, snapping off his surgical glove. "I mean, technically. I'll get you a jar."

Mark tried buckling the jar into the passenger seat but it slipped too much against the belt. It rolled too loose in the glove compartment against the car-care manuals, and so he held it between his legs as he drove, snug against his jean's crotch.

At home, he cradled the jar. The doctor had filled it with a fluid that suspended the mass without dissolving it. Observing the contents, Mark was reminded of a time he went fishing and found himself sitting close to a slop bucket of fins and eyes.

He called his mother. "When you were pregnant with me, did they say you were going to have twins?"

"Of all the items you could have addressed," she replied and hung up.

Though he was proud of it, he didn't want to display the jar on the mantel like a trophy buck. Instead, he placed it on the sill in his kitchen. On fine mornings he enjoyed standing at this window and observing the sparrows on the rail, and now he had a companion.

The afternoon sun caught the curves of glass and sent an array of soft light through the jar and into the room, making both the jar and the room beautiful. It seemed wrong to leave the contents unnamed, as a mass of tissue or a fetus, but equally wrong to give them a kind of birth name, for they had not been born in any traditional sense.

"But you were birthed," Mark said. "I birthed you, and you came to include a jar and an amount of liquid. And so I will call all of you Katherine, after my mother." The cloudy fluid revealed a section of spinal cord floating like a salt-stained twig. Outside, one of the sparrows flung itself into the snow and died.

The winter sun had been kind to Katherine, but the warmth of spring was too aggressive. Mark touched her one morning and found she was warm indeed, enough to be in danger, and so he moved her to his bedside table. She was kept in good company there, alongside his favorite books and that sweet sparrow he had taken immediately to be preserved, wings spread, tipped slightly groundward in the spirit of its final flight. The sparrow's body, elevated on a copper pike, served as a protector of Katherine.

Mark sat up in bed, reading aloud to Katherine and the sparrow. "The poet parted the crowd to approach the loudest man, a worker who had raised his voice out of a professional concern," he said. "The poet clapped his hands on the man's shoulders."

The sparrow's pushpin eyes followed along with the words.

"You go ahead," Mark said.

The sparrow was silent for a moment and then spoke: *Raise high the cathedral walls with oak and pine. Make a church that becomes an ark when turned. Load the ark with men and women and set it to sail. Paint our city in blue and yellow. Paint it to face the sun and sky, paint it to greet the bay.*

"Very good," Mark said. "Very, very good."

He ran his finger gently along the bird's head. Katherine glowed with pride and fluid. Theirs was the happy family he had wanted for five or six days at least.

Mark's mother arrived with the monthly fund. "Katherine, look who's here," he said.

"You break my heart every time you open your mouth," his mother said.

"Well well," he said. "Well well well well well."

"I wish you would take your medicine," she said. "It is trying to kill you. I hate you and I wake up every morning wishing you were dead." She lifted a plastic grocery bag that was of course bulging, as they do. It was not a safe environment, and Katherine right there on the bed. He opened a drawer and tossed its contents at the woman's feet. She trumpeted, the material of her bag grotesque and pooling. A dark fog seeped in under the front door, confounding Mark and the sparrow alike. When the woman was blinded by the fog, Mark pulled off his sweatshirt and wrapped it around Katherine. "I'm straight on," he called out. "I'm straight as a go-dam row." The fog rose like the tide and he gagged in it, finding the woman had become a central part of the fog, that it steamed from her. She went into his body by his mouth and completed a procedure. He held tight to Katherine in her sweatshirt, which had also become Katherine due to principles of matter and transference. "Obviously," he said, sucking the top layers of fog into his mouth and holding them. The sparrow tipped its head above the fog and found its way anew and the sparrow spake: *Once the rhythm is maintained, nothing can pull the orbit askew. We look to Katherine, soft within soft. Katherine, heart aloft, legs tapered reeds. Reigning queen of our bedroom universe. Matriarch and maiden in one, body within body, sourced and pulled free from the whole. Take care to maintain and sustain this tide. Take care!*

Mark's field of vision glowed amber. He returned to find Katherine pressed against his face, her cushion part wrapped protectively around him. Placing her behind him on the bed, he examined the area for danger. Hazards of fog skulked in the corners of the room but the woman was gone.

"Good God, we made it," he said. "We went into it together and came out alive." The bed held Katherine so safely, a raft on silent water, and he saw that she had grown to include the bed as well.

The sparrow on its perch had toppled over in the excitement and landed without ceremony on the floor, its brown feathers gathering sticky dust. It wasn't right.

Katherine floated massive in the room. Mark sat cross-legged beside her on the floor, cradling sparrow and perch. "Fine then," he said, resting his head. She was already deeping down into the planks and spreading across the room, broadening strong along the wood and becoming the lamps and books, the walls, the door.

On the Teat

I curl under my mother's breast and bring my lips to her teat. It gives me comfort to do this and has since before my memory.

She carries me in her arms. Her legs and back and arms are solid from years of this action and there is even a place for me, a divot in her arms and stomach, where my body fits like a shell. I suckle while she speaks of how the span of one's individual memory functions in the same way as a vinyl record, that there is a distinct moment when the needle is placed—by God, she supposes—and the music begins. Assuming all goes well, she says, stroking my hair.

Her own needle was placed forty years ago, at the moment of my conception. I had just begun walking when she first knew my genius. My mind was in a developmental stage akin to a rock rolling down a steep hill, and she was already supplementing my diet with nutrient-rich foods: smoked salmon and handfuls of blueberries, crushed flax. Each morning she gave me a bit of coffee mixed with whole milk. It was all with the idea that she would start the powerful engine early. Breakfast was followed by her special blend of math tutoring and recitation practice, wherein I would recite a poem after each time I had properly summed a fraction. And then our lunch, where she would drink a chilled glass of sugar water and I would lie down and latch easily. Even then I could feel a groove of skin growing in a place under her arm, the fleshy lip hooking over my chest and holding me close. And so the years passed.

I was happy with the life we made, but she decided she wanted to find me a bride. I laughed a little, milk spittling around my mouth, but she didn't return my laughter. She said there would be a time when we could not enjoy these long afternoons and I would be in the world alone. She said her heart broke to think of me out there, wandering. The milk in my mouth took on the salty tinge of the tears she had absorbed.

I said Think of the myth of the pair becoming a tree,

of an old couple looking out the same window while they share a silent song. We have each other.

But not for long, she said.

And so we auditioned prospective girlfriends. They sat on my mother's couch, either too fat or too thin, too pretty or too grotesque. One was focused on the trajectory of her career, while another was practically bovine in her interest in children. A girl played with her hands in her lap, claiming her girlfriends talked her into the whole thing. It was a disaster.

Mother had been making notes in a book, but had taken to facing the wall during the interviews and at the latest girl stopped responding entirely. I told them all to clear out when I saw that she had begun to shudder. I stumbled to her feet, pushing my face into her lap, kneading her stomach and breast like a cat.

She clutched the arms of her chair, quaking so violently it seemed as if a spirit was leaving or entering her. These fucking women, she said. I reached for my divot, blindly trying to soothe her. She pushed me away but I pressed on, wrenching free the buttons of her blouse and drawing her breast roughly into my mouth. She screamed at the pressure of my teeth but quickly calmed and fell asleep in my arms. I held her, dipping my head to reach.

Five

Flight Log, Chicago/Toledo

Smooth air into Chicago this morning. You would have liked it, probably. I mean it would have reminded you of yourself. The sun was rising over the big lake and the captain took the plane around downtown in a circle. We get sick of that kind of view, I mean the captain and I, because after all that splendor we have to bring her down onto some sad tarmac.

———

Everyone thinks I'm drunk these days. Even in the morning. I'm sure you're doing fine.

As the navigating pilot, I felt like it would be fine if we made a nice soft landing in the water, which looked very smooth and dappled from the morning light or similar. That's not something one suggests, of course. It was what we referred to in the Air Force as an internal opinion.

And then from Chicago we headed into Toledo. It's hard to leave Toledo. Just kidding.

I do wonder what the captain is thinking while we're bringing the plane into some place like that where people live their lives. I'm afraid of what he'll say when I ask.

It's probably time to go back to base when every question from the flight attendants inspires me to make the words "Please leave me alone" inside my mouth while my lips are closed while I am smiling and sometimes nodding a little. When you make the words silently, it becomes a secret you can keep. I learned about this in the Air Force.

———

FLIGHT LOG, CHICAGO/TOLEDO

Some nights, I feel I could slip away into a hangar and live in a janitor's closet.

This morning I bought a banana and left it on the counter because I didn't like the look of it. I can't even remember where I was at the time, if you can believe it.

You're such a pretty skeptic.

I'm afraid he'll say he doesn't think of anything at all and then that will make two of us.

I wonder about janitors. If when they close up shop, they go home and clean their own homes. I figure if I was a janitor I would pop a squat on the floor and make a watery BM every now and again to keep myself humble.

What do you do to keep yourself humble? You'll have to remind me because I can't think of a goddammed thing.

Loop

You are one man standing barefoot in a grocery store. You regard rows of snack-cake cartons stacked like bricks when your mind begins to go. You knew it in your heart: Your heart is a wall of the same brick repeated. You're standing barefoot because you put your slippers into the coffee bulk bin where they make like rabbit ears and listen up.

At home, you call your mom and her voice reminds you of a pancake you dropped on the floor that morning. Because you have no dog, you got on your hands and knees and ate that pancake up off the floor. You licked your lips and the floor and took a nap in your nap spot.

You tell your mom you don't remember her wearing a lot of denim. Your mom corrects you and says she did wear more denim than you remember. She says, Your father worked in denim. Your crib was made of denim. He covered it for your safety. Every problem can be traced to attention or its lack. As your mom goes on you watch a video that features a woman facing the camera and talking about yoga, and her nipples straining her costume are themselves talking in a sea tone of the responsibility of owning animals.

As you watch the video for the tenth time you work your way down the numbers in your Casual Encounters file but each call receives no answer. You try one number again and again until a bird picks up and tells you to fuck-right-off, fuck-right-off. Your heart is a wall of the same brick repeated.

A man returns your call and asks if you're the guy who wants a visit. Says he knows a guy, knows a lot of guys actually and some women, that every one of them knows a thing or two about bricks and they're all coming over.

You have been surrounded all your life by people concerned for your health. Men build scaffolding to protect your stupid skull. Cars stop and allow you to cross. Every problem in the world can be traced to attention or its lack.

The man arrives at your door wearing some serious denim. You carry a folding chair and follow him down the steps to the alley. He has assembled a crowd. He produces an awl and taps it around the circumference of your neck. Checking out, he says. I've had my days and yours aren't my business.

You can't feel it. The man tells the crowd That's all, folks. He angles it in the nape of your neck. He is a magician. You smile for the crowd. Your heart's a wall. Your heart is a wall.

Mom calls, but the man is tapping his awl beside your ear and you can only hear her saying denim denim denim, denim denim. Denim denim. Den-den-denim-denim. Denim. Den-den. Denim-um. Denum. Denumm. Den-den-den-den. Um. Umm. Um-um.

Your collarbone crk-crks and is liberated. The man in denm is whistlin "Home on the Range." Word lip saside. Yu make a momont to fleck on the lean of the nalley, the pn sponch & yr hart it's a wallv th sambrick repeetd, th snik-snik, th sm-brk, rpt-rpt-rpt.

Thank You

The woman checked her mail every afternoon. One day, she found a card from her friend. The card, pale green and decorated with filigrees and flowers, was lovely. Inside, the woman's friend had written a sweet note, thanking the woman for a baby-shower gift she had sent from a catalog.

"Such a beautiful card," said the woman, turning it over. She wanted to show her appreciation for the sentiment presented and the effort implied, given that her friend was quite pregnant and still thought to sit down and write a heartfelt note in a darling card.

The woman sat down at her desk and opened the drawer, extracting a few options. One card was festive, with holly sprigs and a touch of glitter. Another featured a nautical stripe and a jaunty anchor. The woman, feeling the season appropriate, chose the first. She picked a fresh pen and wrote: "Thank you for your kind thank-you card. I appreciate so much that you considered our friendship this month, and I so look forward to meeting the new addition to your family. All my love."

She signed her name, addressed and stamped an envelope, slipped the card inside, and dropped it in the mail.

Some days passed, and the woman received another letter. Inside its sturdy envelope, the cream-colored card was embossed with her friend's name on the front and inside that, with the woman's name. The woman gasped with delight and sat down in her office to read: "Thank you, my dear, for the thoughtful thank-you card in response to my thank-you card. It pleased me greatly to see your response, as I count you among my most polite friends. Yours."

Such a thoughtful gesture! She immediately picked a card from her drawer; this one was sunny yellow, with four butterflies in a line. Inside, she wrote: "Thank you for your thank-you card recognizing my thank-you card for your thank-you card. We are truly friends."

This returned sentiment seemed slightly less personal and the woman panicked before remembering the small craft supply she kept for her children to play with when she worked late. She uncapped a tube of silver glitter and deposited a healthy quarter cup into the envelope before inserting the card. She dropped it in the mail and went to bed.

Eight days later, a brown paper package arrived. The woman took it up to her room. Inside, she found a handful of bright cherry bombs and a decorative plate, on which her friend had painted the words THANK YOU. The woman lit a cherry bomb, threw it into her bathtub, and watched it crack merrily about, thinking of her friend's thoughtful nature.

The woman spent the afternoon assembling supplies to make a chocolate cake. She waited patiently for it to cool before she piped raspberry cream between the layers and at the base. She found a box that would fit the cake and tore out the pages of five of her favorite books, running them through the shredder to make a nest for the cake to travel on. Discovering she was out of pastry cream, she wrote THANKS on an empty paper towel roll and affixed it to the frosting. By the time the postman picked it up the next morning, a fluid had condensed, leaving a sticky ring on the mailroom floor.

She began to have trouble sleeping. A postal tube arrived and she opened it to release eight disoriented white mice. They tumbled out in a line and scrambled for safety. She gave them water and sliced up an apple but was confused by their presence until later that evening when, save for one, they seized and made tiny bowel movements that respectively produced alphabet beads T H A N K O and U.

The last mouse was uncomfortably constipated in a life-threatening way until she took him to the vet and had the Y extracted at the expense of forty-five dollars.

A fever gripped the woman and she was bound to her bed for a week. When she could walk again, she set immediately to work. She mixed industrial buckets of yellow lye, loaded them up after dark, and drove to the park, which featured swings for children and a community garden and a broad green lawn.

In the morning she set up an old VCR to record the news and drank coffee while she rebandaged her chemical burns. They came in live from the grassy field. There was a clip of the landscape men being piled into the back of a police truck, one of them crying. There was a good live shot of the THANKS on the grass still smoking comically from burned patches. There was talk of reevaluating local law enforcement, of adding cameras. She popped the tape in the mail that afternoon.

The following week, the woman opened her door to find a baby boy in a basket. The infant was too small to speak but the woman knew exactly what he would say when he did.

Legacy

Keepers here are required to do more than trim and water the plots, make a note of sinking or cracking, seed bare patches, feed the peacocks, and feed the cats. This is the last piece of luxury property most people ever own apart from acquisitions in the afterlife, and so there're a few special things we do to make the investment worth it. The slings and trappings all find their way here. We know how to treat such matters with respect.

You'll recall the pharaohs were entombed with whatever they wanted to hang on to: usually women and cats, pots of honey. These days, we might pour in a shipping crate of golf balls before nestling the linksman into the dimpled rough and covering him up with a soft layer of tees. We had a starlet request her casket be filled with vodka, the good stuff. We floated her in it like an olive and locked it down. She didn't spring for watertight, though; for five months, the grass wouldn't grow. We had to lay down plastic turf.

A tax man had a crate of mice scattered through his mourners so he could be entombed with the sense of panic he inspired. A ballet instructor wanted her students to pas de bourrée in the grave to tamp down the soil before she was placed. We got the girls out before their teacher was lowered in, but for a little extra, who knows—maybe we would have looked away, have one of them do a solo piece while we backed in the dirt.

There was the assistant, beloved by all on the lot next door, who was placed in a grave we left unmarked but for a stone bench so his boss could sit and yell *Martin! Get on the fucking call!* and similar for many glad hours. The studio even financed a granite letter tray. Every full moon, they say, a ghostly figure deposits three duplicates of a contract to be sent to Legal.

People ask about the rock stars. Are they all mix tapes and pinners? Is the crypt packed with roses? These are secrets we keep. We surround folks with what they put a lot of energy and effort into, a lot of value. It might be color wheels of gel acrylics, letters from old friends. A nice layer of cash. Every body of work deserves its spoils. When we keepers go, we'll get maps and plans and cenotaphs in miniature, all housed deep under slabs bearing the names of every man, woman, and blue-faced baby we drew down, a towering monument to our work.

So come in, look around. Slip off your shoes, test the soil. Visit the peacocks and their dowdy hens. Take a seat under a tree and speculate to nobody in particular about exactly what, when your ship has sailed, you would like to take below deck. It might seem like a lonely afternoon there in the shade, but take heart; we'll be listening.

The Man Ahead

A wrong turn threw Jim off the route. He took a slow circle around a dead end and headed back, falling in behind a
line of cars. The man ahead took a right and Jim followed,
seeking the highway. A jetting spray shot from the man's
windshield just as Jim's finger stretched for the wipers and
they worked in tandem again. Jim found he could focus
and learn precisely what the man ahead was planning and
copy him exactly with hardly a half-second delay. He
followed close to confirm: indeed, he signaled early and
drifted to the left just after the man ahead, who took a sip

of coffee the instant Jim thought to lift his travel mug. They both half glanced at the highway as it slipped by. The man ahead moved to pass a bus, and though he could have made pace beside, Jim kept slightly behind. From these few one-sided exchanges, Jim was surprised to find the satisfaction that his life had found some small but valid purpose. The feeling was exhilarating.

After a brisk route past a long line of warehouses, the man ahead pulled into a parking lot. Jim parked in a spot behind and followed him into the building, where they each gave a cursory nod to the guard at the front desk. In the small elevator, Jim felt compelled to stand behind the man but very close, with his nose almost but not quite touching the man's shoulder. They breathed together.

The maze of cubicles offered no obvious navigational clues, and Jim was relieved that the man ahead knew where to go. Trying to memorize the route by landmarks—a large printer on the right, a board pinned with blank pages, a glass-walled meeting room, a large printer on the left—proved too complex. Jim kept a brisk pace and they both came to a stop in front of a woman, who minimized a picture of a motorcycle.

"The meeting got pushed," she said.

"Thank God," said the man ahead. Jim said, "Thank God."

The woman frowned at Jim and returned her attention to the man. "You'll have a little extra time to work on the deck. Did you swap out the copy I sent?"

"On the first page, yeah," said the man ahead, and Jim, starting "On" when the man had gotten to "first," made a quick repeat.

"You have a shadow today," the woman said.

The man made a move to turn—stiffly, as if he had a sore neck—and shrugged without comment.

"We really need this done in an hour," she said. "I owe you one."

"I'll get you something soon," he said, and "—soon" echoed.

Work went quickly; surprising for the fact that without a chair or desk of his own, Jim was forced to squat and pantomime the actions of keyboard and mouse. He found strength in his quadriceps and a real sense of humor about the situation. The monochrome details of his own morning and afternoon had been replaced entirely by this man's desires and obligations. At lunch, they ate a tuna salad sandwich, Jim's in pantomime but with no less appreciation for the atmosphere of the lunch hour. There was a communal depression in the lunchroom, but Jim was not affected by it; rather, he experienced a feeling akin to walking past an old mattress leaning against a building. He was a tourist here and would move on soon to other scenic spots.

After work, the man ahead drove to an apartment complex. Jim had figured out a rhythm to their movement and never faltered on the commute; he may as well have been in the man's backseat. Pedestrians stepping into the road no longer saw Jim; they saw only the man ahead.

In the apartment, the man kissed a woman and Jim followed so quickly, leaning in to brush her cheek with his lips, she didn't notice him at all.

"Where were you?" she asked.

"At work," he said, "work."

"Yesterday, I mean."

"I was—" he said, "was—"

"They said you'd called in sick, so let's cut the story." She was wearing a housedress, but Jim saw the shape of her body underneath and wanted to place his hand on the curve of her hip. He felt an absorption into the man ahead and experienced in that moment a series of memories of sexual experiences, including but not limited to placing his left index finger into a woman's vagina and the feeling of pressing his face between a pair of breasts until his nose felt crushed against her sternum. These feelings were at once striking and then dull. They mirrored the way he experienced his own memories, as if they were a dancer who rushed to the edge of the stage and then retreated.

"You have to be honest with me," she said, letting them touch her. "It's important we're in a partnership here."

"Of course-se."

He reached for her. When their three hands touched, the man and woman jolted and drew back, staring at Jim.

"I—" Jim faltered.

"What the hell," said the man.

"What the hell?" Jim said, but it was all off.

The woman looked at her door and at Jim and back at

the door, which was locked. Jim knew he had one chance. "Please," he said. "Don't give up."

They sat for a moment together. The other man placed his hand atop Jim's. "Please, don't give up," he said to the woman.

"I'm not," the woman said.

"Good," Jim said.

"Good," said the man.

They left her there, the other man a step behind. Outside, Jim looked to the cars lined up on the highway. "Let's go," he said. "We have places to be."

"Let's go," said the man.

You know the rest.

House Proud

It's harder to leave your burning home after you've spent so much time cleaning its floors. Watching those baseboards char should be enough to make any good woman lie back in bed and let it happen. The fact that I got up and hauled Angela out with me is proof enough of my selfishness.

The years with her father before the fire—when I still had my figure and the energy to walk about, the will and ability to be moved—passed with such seeming ease, but the truth of those days and the trouble they held is lost in the archives of memory's drunken catalog. Its delicate, age-soaked pages stay with me like an old phone book packed and moved out of some sentimental urge.

If anyone has found an adequate response to that fiction of chemical and circumstance which is love, it is my Angela. Even when she was a girl, she squirmed out of my grasp and kissed the kitchen table instead. She was barely toddling and would force me with pleads and screaming to spend hours on the bridge over the county road, tucking flowers between its wooden slats.

She shrank into a child's malaise when they demolished the old post office. The workers had dumped the remnants of the structure and covered it with a few buckets of sand, and she wept and reached for it. This wasn't her usual brand of sadness, the kind she had when her blanket was tumbling in the dryer and she could only watch from her crib, a few sweet tears on her cheek. At the pile, she was hysterical. I let her down and she stumbled toward it, tripping over her feet, grinding dirt into her hands and face, ruining her play clothes. She kicked and crawled, wailing, scrabbling at the pile until finally her fingers found purchase. She took hold and leaned back with her full weight, wrenching a brick free and inspiring a plume of dirt. A man walking down the road stopped and stared. She cleared the brick from the pile, covered it with her body, and was asleep by the time I approached. I couldn't remove it without waking her and so brought it home with us, the thing weighing her down in her car seat. I remember it was warm, the brick. At home, I wrapped it in a sheet of newspaper and left it on the dresser beside her crib.

She took on a mighty insomnia, reaching always for the brick. A neighbor suggested the pediatric hospital downtown. I considered an appointment but couldn't bear to think of them running tests on a little girl who had merely cried over a pile of building materials. She was too sensitive and thoughtful, easy to tears and infant rages. This could all mean strength and character in adulthood, but any doctor would return with her simple imbalances marked on a chart. He would never wonder if something is not simply born into a person with no reason or requirement. Her father would have agreed. And so I put the brick in her crib with her and she slept soundly. From my chair, in which I spent only the evening hours of those new days, I sipped my drink and strained my ears to the strange sound of her silence.

My darling girl fattened into a woman but never truly recovered from the malaise which distinguished her as a child. She took the room above mine when it opened up in the duplex and brought my dinner down every night. My sensibilities lean to the fish fry and hot dish. A dessert of mine once took first in the neighborhood fair after I took the boxed brownie mix and added chopped up Mars bars; all the ladies did it that way after that. I appreciate her, but truly she is dull in the kitchen.

My bacon was always crisp, my roast chicken a celebration of subtle spice. Meanwhile, she microwaves her meats to the consistency of a hot rubber wheel. She substitutes rice for butter because of its similar shade. She keeps her potatoes for hours in boiling water, creating a soup she must strain before she dishes up the slop.

She served me a plate of canned beans on a piece of white bread and told me it was a recipe she found on the television.

"What television are you watching?"

"We should go to the tower," she said, settling into the couch beside me, moving my oxygen tank to make room for her feet. I fantasize about being rid of the couch; I never much cared for the lack of material distinction from the lesser piece of furniture, preferring to think of my recliner as a velveteen rose throne rather than part of a living room set. "The tower is my lover."

The boundary between bean and bread had vanished, and truly the mixture had creamed under its own power. "Fine, fine," I said. "But what television?"

She was kind enough to drive me places. I'm a little delicate these days, despite my size, and time away from my recliner wears me out. I only go to meetings anymore. The bones shift in my body like those in a creature dead under ice. They weaken slightly more each time I stand to share my story of sweet hidden booze and the personal redemption that came with a will toward freedom.

I had to reach for a man while I was speaking on how my higher power is represented by the face of Angela's father and my father combined. As I spoke, I felt a blindness creep. I sank across the aisle of folding chairs and the young man caught me under my arms as if he had been anticipating the chance. Surely he was placed there. My vision was crowded with fire; the tube had crimped inside its case, we learned later. I clutched at him and swayed, listening to the feeling that resonated into sound within my bones. I felt their air thin, and so held this man, waiting for the scene to clear and reveal again the circle of chairs and their assorted old-timers. Over cold coffee after, the man said he was new in town and agreed he would try to make it over sometime for dinner and that he could bring a pan of his gram's cornbread, in which the secret was canned corn. In the car, Angela closed her architecture magazine and cheerily asked me what the drunks went on about this time.

She brought me milk cloudy with water for my breakfast, first claiming it was a diet tonic but, once pressed, admitted she only had the dregs of a carton left in her house and no other food at all. Worse, as she sat and watched me drink it, I spied a wet bit of fried egg trembling in her hair. She jerked back when I tried to pick it out, and so I took hold of her shirtsleeve and told her to let me smell it on her breath, at which point she called me an occultist and left the house with the door unlocked. It took a great effort for me to drag the tank and stop and lean on it and drag the tank again and finally reach and bolt the door, because I was not well and I remain not well. The tank leaned me solicitous toward the floor, but I knew that it would be the end of me if I fell, and so I dragged it back to my chair, where I drifted in and out of a sad doze. My tank whirred to an eventual halt and my child did not return for some time, during which I resorted to scraping and licking dishes within reach, gasping like a fish. I like to keep my feet in a tub, but even the water gave me no comfort once it turned gray and cold. I had no strength to change it and so I kicked it over like a mule and wept.

She returned the following Saturday without explanation or apology, bearing a plate of beef jerky, which she balanced ceremoniously in my lap.

"I want to take you to my lover," she said.

"It is not possible."

"But you'll be so proud."

I was breathing easier since she hooked in a new tank but I was still very weak. The ribbed fabric of my short nightgown had branded my legs and I tried to rub the pattern away with my thumb. A knob of jerky landed in the mess of wet newspaper at my feet. She reached down and retrieved the meat, drying it on her jeans and placing it before me, brushing away a fly.

"I take you to your meetings," she said. "I brought you a new tank."

"There's no effort in it."

"You should come with me to meet my lover."

Leaving the house requires a week's worth of strength and still she makes this request.

"A man came by. I heard him knocking on your door

and then he came up and knocked on mine. I saw him through the peephole."

"And then you let him in? You invited him to sit with you and watch television? Your hands inched across the couch toward each other in the heady first days of love?"

"I didn't take the chain off the door and he left. There was a pan of cornbread on your mat. It was fine." She made an idiotic little half smile and shrugged.

"Certainly all of it was fine."

"Mother, you are on a diet."

"Certainly!"

"You should get on your feet and take a little exercise. Come with me to see my lover."

"You certainly are doing just fine."

It took me a few hours after she was gone to calm down, but I eventually decided that her happiness, though fleeting and confused, and alienated from the love and comfort of others, is still happiness, and I should be glad and grateful. Her old raffia beach bag had sprinkled stray gravel when she lifted it to go and I saw enough of it studding the rug to ruin the vacuum.

I've earned the right to sit after years on my feet. I started in my teen years as a cashier at the sporting goods store, feeling the blood struggle to work its circuit back up my system. It was more of the same at the chalkboard, incanting grammatical clauses, ankles swollen so thick that they looked ready to give birth to a pair of screaming children that would match the ones I served. Whole afternoons were lost tracing the edge of the road from home to school and from school back home, shivering against the trucks, toddling in stupid shoes that inspired knots, my flask warm all the while against my thigh. I leaned like a pack beast against walls and doorframes, waiting for the day to end. I stood beside my man at the altar, stood to save our child from the fire, and stood to hold her while she fussed and puked, whispering in her ear that the sitter was stealing from us. Sleep was a horizontal version of the same; I braced my feet against a pillow, standing in my dreams. And so, yes, when the work was over and with it the requirement of mobility, I sat immediately and with satisfaction. I wore out folding chairs and sofa cushions and then I found my velveteen rose, my reinless ride, and I did take my throne and fuse its plush to my own and from it for the remainder of my days I will Ride.

Angela returned the next morning, refilled the tub for my feet, and fed me pieces of ham. When I was through, she wiped up the mess of magazines and soiled clothing, working without complaint. I was suspicious.

"Would you like a ride to the early meeting?" she asked.

"That would be so kind."

"I value you truly."

"And I you, darling." We were a mother and daughter in a stage play. I took her wrists, which limped in my grasp. She twitched and she made a chuffing sound. I thought she was angry with me, but she was gentle with my tubes as she loaded me into the car.

At meeting, the young man who had caught me before smiled and sat on the far end of the room. I waited
patiently until it was my time to share.

"My child should be grateful for the life she has been
afforded through my sacrifice and work," I said. "She should
be thankful for my loving control, optimistic for the years
ahead. There are cultures in which the daughter is tied to
the mother for her entire adult life, physically bound with
a rope, released only for the carnal act, and then the two
are bound together again. You'll find a maternal lineage of
women going through the streets like that, and when one
slows to observe a basket of peaches, they all stop and make
a group decision on the merits of the greengrocer. Com-
pared to that, we seem so distant as to be almost strangers."

A young woman applauded, laughing. I pitied her,
forced to dry out in a lonesome apartment, opening tinned
food for cats, slicing a peach for her own dinner and eating it over a sink facing the wall. She makes much of her
own bravery but has no one to be brave for, and when she
dies, her old cat will pluck out her eye. She will be found
by a landlord collecting his rent.

At night I think of my child above me, my husband
above her, and my old smiling Higher Power above them
both, and I say: *Keep this girl hidden out of the light so that her
eyes may become wide dark voids that might better reflect me.*

Angela came bearing a box of doughnuts and handed me
one on a plate. A fly had been troubling my legs all morning
and this was a happy departure. She talked of a memorable

television program, digging into her bag as she went on, the snapped straw at its corners ripping her stockings when it grazed her leg. Her lovely dark hair was matted and her right knee was roseate with a blooming bruise. The contents of her bag threatened to emerge: a pilled sweater; three or four notebooks; disposable chopsticks in their paper; the parched nub of a carrot. Surely there was a wallet in there, some identification, her old first-aid card. A package of gum, stale and somehow rumpled. She extracted a fork and set it on my plate as the fly landed on the doughnut, plunging its sucker mouth.

"Eat your breakfast," she said, glancing up from her bag for only a moment. The skin around her eyes was cracked at the edges like she was carved from clay. I would keep her under glass if I could. She found a dried mass of facial tissue, honked into it, and examined the evidence. The fly rubbed its spindled legs together and placed them on the doughnut, a chocolate-frosted variety.

"I wish you would ride with me to my lover," she said.

I took a healthy bite. The fly tried valiantly to extract itself from where it was trapped, and the ticklish sensation inside my mouth started me laughing. "Where?" I asked.

She regarded my laughter. "Not too far."

That damn fly invigorated me.

"In the woods," she said.

"All right then, before I change my mind."

She clasped her hands and kissed me on the cheek. If

I had been able to reach the picture of her father on the mantel, I would have turned it to face the wall.

This drive would be longer, she said, and we needed to prepare. It took some time in the car to wedge the spare tank under my legs, and once we figured that out, the glove compartment popped open and wagged against my belly. She drove us to the edge of town, past the county school and the new junkyard, a handful of ranches, the regional airport, and the place where the community college took their cadaver dogs out to train them.

She spun the wheel a couple of minutes after we passed the old junkyard and we jagged off the road onto a gravel path. She shifted into a lower gear as we bounced over the road, which transitioned to dirt in short order. My body groaned with the jostling and I gripped the dash.

She had to keep up a pace fast enough that we wouldn't sink. A colorful series of pennants were strung up, the kind from a party store, and she turned there and pressed on. I wondered at how she got out here in the first place. The glove compartment unlatched again on a significant bump and out spilled cassette tapes and receipts and a travel guide to Oklahoma.

"You are going to destroy your alignment," I murmured to the mess.

At that moment she stopped the car so violently I

thought that she was angry with me, then she ran us into a log and took out the engine entirely. But then she put it in park and trotted around to let me out. "Come on," she said.

We were parked at the unceremonious end of a trail, foliage on three of four sides. She had taken us as far as we could go. Another bright line of flags was strung across a low branch. The pennants read CONGRATULATION, the s tied around the tree. She headed for the woods but turned back before she rounded the bend. "Come on," she repeated.

My shirt rode up when I leaned against the exterior of the car, and the moisture condensed below my shirt and soaked through the elastic edge of my pants and onto the broad plain of their jersey fabric.

"How far is it?"

"We came all this way. Just over the ridge."

Walking was an insult to my condition. This was my only child, knowing the pain I was in and forcing me to go pursue that pain for some silent third party. This was the first time we had been at this impasse, and my heart sank at the idea that it would not be the last. Still, I obeyed. My ankles moaned against the intrusion of unstable ground, but I obeyed. The terrain soaked cold through my soft shoes. Shards of stone cut into my feet as I lurched toward my baby girl.

"Watch your footing," she said, though she knew it was enough work already to make progress up the hill. She knew. She wrapped her arms around me when I reached her. I thought for a hopeful moment that she might carry me on her back. Her big bag fell against me, a comforting sudden weight. We held each other.

"There you are," she whispered, squeezing. My breath caught and seized.

We walked what felt like a twisting mile through the dale. Every step reminded me of my chair and I longed for it. I thought of dinner and sleep, I thought of gin. My ankles ached but it was my bones that truly troubled me. They locked and ground. I remembered a doctor cautioning me against activity, displaying a model of a normal leg and then removing some key elements, pushing the remaining bones together to demonstrate my future. There among the soaked and rotting wood I felt the doctor's hands on my own legs and feet, twisting them as he watched my expression. I tried to conjure an image of my dear husband to busy my mind but could see only his bones as we cleared the ridge.

She had spoken of a tower. I thought it would crest the hill, a fortress against the sun, abounding stone, room enough for horses. Instead, I was faced with a broken place. The walls were charred to a cold crisp, its slate roof sagging, windows burst and gone, the door a seared gape. It sat alone in an airless glade, four simple walls ringed with a fading constellation of ash. Her great love was a ruin like any other.

The homesteader who built the place must have wanted dearly to be alone. He built far from any path, choosing an area flanked by boulders and fallen trees as if he hoped to dissuade even the limber animals who might otherwise discover the clearing. The trees bending deferent seemed to be shielding the unhappy space from errant light and the setting sun managed only to cast a dark purple wash across the ruined place, giving it the look of a drowned man.

"It burned," she said. "Before I knew it."

She walked ahead, arms swinging with purpose. I could not quite hear what she was saying and realized she was speaking to the house. She touched its threshold frame. I had a vision of the place aflame, its slate a foreign sky. She rubbed her soot-black fingers together before dropping to her knees like she was looking under a bed. She pressed her face against the wall. I heard her groan. My tank bounced on the terrain as I worked toward her and then passed her in the threshold.

Inside, it was warm and dark against the wind. Ash made a drifting slope in each corner. There was a trapped energy in the walls as if the ghost of the fire remained to charge it. If my chair was placed here, it would serve to complete a dark circuit.

And there, knees muddling the char, my girl kissed the brick. I watched despite my disgust, for what mother can truly stand to see her child in love. Hunched there on the ground, she licked and gagged, whimpering as sweetly as when she nursed from my breast.

Dragging my tank through blooming ash, I moved to her side. I leaned down and felt my spine jag in on itself, air bubbling from its subtle pores. I fell to one knee and then the other. The tube sprang from my nose and went spiraling into darkness. I crawled to my child where she lay, tonguing the wall. I gripped her, sensing her father with us there. I felt his disappointment in me.

"It's perfect," I said, wrapping my arms around her, mouth to her ear as her face pressed the wall. We collapsed and curled around each other on the ground, our breath a union, in no place like home.

Acknowledgments

Thanks are owed to Emily Bell at FSG and the whole team: Elizabeth Gordon, Karla Eoff, Justine Gardner, Ellen Feldman, Abby Kagan, Adrienne Davis, and Debra Helfand. Thanks also to the editors who published parts of this work prior to collection and whose thoughts helped shape this whole, particularly those who gave substantive notes: Emma Komlos-Hrobsky at *Tin House*, Ben Marcus at *The American Reader*, Cal Morgan at *52 Stories*, Jordan Bass at *McSweeney's*, Michael Barron at New Directions, Tim Small at *VICE*, Drew Burk at *Spork*, Jesse Pearson at *Apology*, Matt Williamson at *Unstuck*, and Amber Sparks for Melville House. Thanks to Claudia Ballard for her devotion, Lauren Goldstein for her thoughts, Lee Shipman for his love and support, and to my family, near and far.